THE STONE
OF TRUTH

It was a seven-sided crystal the size of an egg, which pulsed with a light of its own, a cool blue iridescence. The light bathed me and suddenly I saw the universe. Now I was seeing the Truth itself. I knew. I understood. The world I lived in was a dream, a workable fabric of concepts. This peak, this crater, this pool of lava, all insubstantial, ephemeral. The Truth was a web of brilliant connecting fibers. Golden ropes of power. The fibers formed a nexus at the power stone clutched in my fist, and fanned off in every direction. One of the fibers connected to me— I was part of it!

And then the power called to me and I went. . . .

The Best in Science Fiction from SIGNET

The
Secrets
of
SYNCHRONICITY

by
Jonathan Fast

A SIGNET BOOK
NEW AMERICAN LIBRARY
TIMES MIRROR

For Erica

Higher peace, higher truth, higher universe

NAL BOOKS ARE ALSO AVAILABLE AT DISCOUNTS IN BULK
QUANTITY FOR INDUSTRIAL OR SALES-PROMOTIONAL USE.
FOR DETAILS, WRITE TO PREMIUM MARKETING DIVISION,
NEW AMERICAN LIBRARY, INC., 1301 AVENUE OF THE
AMERICAS, NEW YORK, NEW YORK 10019.

 SIGNET TRADEMARK REG. U.S. PAT. OFF. AND FOREIGN COUNTRIES
REGISTERED TRADEMARK—MARCA REGISTRADA
HECHO EN CHICAGO, U.S.A.

SIGNET, SIGNET CLASSICS, MENTOR, PLUME AND MERIDIAN BOOKS
are published by The New American Library, Inc.,
1301 Avenue of the Americas, New York, New York 10019

FIRST SIGNET PRINTING, JULY, 1977

3 4 5 6 7 8 9

PRINTED IN THE UNITED STATES OF AMERICA

My example concerns a young woman patient . . . She had had an impressive dream the night before, in which someone had given her a golden scarab—a costly piece of jewellery. While she was still telling me this dream, I heard something behind me gently tapping on the window. I turned around and saw that it was a fairly large flying insect . . . It was a scarabaeid beetle . . . whose gold-green color most nearly resembles that of a golden scarab.

—C. G. Jung, *On Synchronicity*

Alchemy was the distinctive form taken by magic in the seventeenth century; the Philosopher's Stone (or *Lapis*) it sought was nothing less than man's ultimate control over death . . .

The secret sought by the alchemists was, according to Jung, the secret of the transmutation *of consciousness* into the godlike state . . . He associated it also with the aim of the Yogis—and it is significant that unusual "powers" over matter are regarded by Hindus as a natural byproduct of the spiritual transformation of the yogi—as with the alchemists.

—Colin Wilson, *The Occult*

Part I

Escape from Slabour

Without stepping out of your door
You may know the ways of man,
Without looking out of your window
You may know the ways of heaven.
The farther one travels, the less one knows.
　　　　　—Holy Tapes of the Bode-Satva
　　　　　　(Tape #29,471)

1

I crawled into the mines of Slabour as I had every morning since arriving on this bald barren asteroid three long years ago when I was fifteen. But this morning was different—I had a plan to escape.

I was not a prisoner of manacles and chains, no, I was a wage slave and had become one of my own free will, through my own ignorance and stupidity.

My dad was playing the Daily Tape during breakfast, watching the words race across the screen, scanning the classifieds, when an ad caught my eye:

> BOYS! DON'T MISS THIS EXCITING OFFER!
> A MAJOR CORPORATION WILL SEND *YOU* ON
> AN ALL-EXPENSE-PAID ROUND TRIP SPACE
> FLIGHT TO . . .

After he left for work I replayed the ad with growing excitement. A free trip to a far corner of the galaxy in return for six weeks' labor!

I was bored with school, angry at being forced to do chores— "to build character" —while the domestic robots gathered rust. I'd never been off the planet, and space sang me a siren's song of adventure.

That evening I told my folks what I wanted to do. My dad forbade me; I knew he would. He said he'd heard about such offers and they always had a catch. Hard work, that was the way. Hard work in school, and when I graduated I could get a job anywhere in the galaxy. It would only be a few more years.

But my mother was wiser. She grew sad and silent, for she knew that once I'd made up my mind there was no stopping me. I'd always been headstrong, more susceptible to dare than doubt, more proud than prudent.

Late that night I climbed down the trellis beneath my bedroom window; then into town on the porta-walk, then the tube to the cityplex spaceport, all while they slept unaware. I imagined them calling me to breakfast. Running upstairs, my empty sleep-slab. Reading the note I left behind, then televideoing the police.

By that time I was buckled into my lounger, awaiting liftoff.

How I longed to see the Milky Way sparkling like a diamond crown, and the pinwheel fireworks of the nebulae! But the converted freighter we shipped in had no viewports. I'd wake up in my hammock screaming from dreams of falling and vomit up the nutra-foods and sedatives until finally they had to put me in slo-doz. It was not at all like the space adventures I'd seen on tapes.

Then the tiny asteroid called Slabour. They took me to the top of the administration tower for processing, and I could see through the windows 360 degrees of horizon. It looked like a rusty coin, cracked and pitted. The sky, an artificial atmosphere, was the color of dry blood. The rust-red dust from the clay did that. It burned the eyes, clogged the nose and made a gritty taste in the mouth and a wheeze in the lungs. As for the mines—I was never so glad to be small and skinny and unafraid of tight places.

I vowed that when the six weeks were up I would ship home and be the most obedient of sons. I would do chores and study hard with never a word of complaint. And never again would I be seduced by the lure of space.

I hadn't counted on expenses.

At the end of the first week one of the security guards brought me a bill for 200 credit units. Room and board. The food was shipped in from Romine 3, that was why it was so expensive. Well, I had on me precisely twenty-eight CUs, my carefully hoarded allowance.

So I went to the tower, to talk to Boss Callow. He said if I traded in my return passage for credit, he would take me on as a regular Digger and pay me a salary. When I'd saved enough I could buy back my passage home.

I put my name on a contract cassette. But I never saved any money. Aside from the room and board, there were other expenses. Showers, lixor, a new pair of coveralls—I wore through the knees every few weeks—and the scru-shed.

At first I stayed away from there. I'd never had a woman before and I was afraid though I made believe I just wasn't interested. Then one night Simon and Mo got me numb on lixor and carried me down to the scru-shed and bought me a Scrugal named Suki who called me her big brave spaceman. I never told them, but that first night I lay in her arms and cried and cried. She stroked my head and whispered things, like my mom used to do when I was little.

It wasn't until later that week that I loved her. She made me feel like I was king of the heavens—not just another Digger. Sometimes, when we weren't in the mood for loving, we would be content to talk, or play a game of speckers. We were both awful cheats. I'd be winning and she'd say, "Stefin, will you look at that!" When I turned my head to see what was so interesting, she rearranged the pieces. Then she looked all coy and innocent, and pretended to be fixing her hair. After a few more moves, I pointed out something behind her and I put the pieces back the way they were. Then we rolled around on the air-cot, giggling that two grown people could be so silly.

At the end of that month Suki and the other Scrugals were shipped away and a new bunch took their place. I still went to the scru-shed but I never met another I liked as much as her.

That was three years ago but I remember her distinctly. She had the softest saddest eyes, like smudges of charcoal. She didn't smile much, and when she did it was a very special present. The black hair which fell in ringlets to her shoulders looked, in a certain light, blue. She had a slim figure and long graceful legs. I thought about her a lot.

2

We were hiking to the barracks after a day of digging and I knew something was up because Simon and Mo kept grinning at me.

"What is it with you dumb diggers?" I asked, irritated.

"We thought we'd go down to the scru-shed," Simon said. "Want to come along?"

Simon was nineteen, one of the oldest Diggers and certainly

the cleverest. He was tall and skinny and bent from the mines, with a big crooked nose and an Adam's apple that stuck out almost as far.

"I don't think so," I said. "I'm finally starting to save a little money," I added, for an excuse.

He mimicked me pretty well. "By the time I'm 281 I expect I'll have a passage home."

Mo looked puzzled. His jaw hung slack, as was his habit when he tried to think.

"How can you save till you're 281? Nobody lives that long."

Simon explained and eventually Mo got the point and laughed and laughed. That was one of the things I liked about Simon. Anybody else would have told Mo he was an idiot and left it at that, but Simon cared. In the beginning Mo had been no dumber than the rest of us—which was often pretty dumb—but then a mine ceiling had collapsed on his head and since then he'd been a little dumber.

"Please come with us." Mo spoke slowly, slurring his words. "There's somebody who wants to surprise—"

"Hush, Mo," Simon interrupted. "It's no surprise if you tell."

Well, that got me so curious, I couldn't say no.

In the barracks I peeled off my coveralls and started for the shower. It isn't easy crossing a hut filled with three hundred Diggers just back from the mines. The smell is asphyxiating until the ventilation system goes to work on it. And the chaos is enough to make you want to eat clay. Everybody is screaming and wrestling and jumping around—that's what you do after eight hours in a hole where the ceiling's so low you can't straighten your back. Some of the older Diggers like myself comported themselves maturely, but the little kids acted like maniacs. I sympathized—I remembered what it was like—but now I wanted to get to the shower, and when a little kid jumped off his hammock and landed on top of me, I gave him a poke.

I shouldn't have been so rough. He was Sennel-Rey, a wispy tow-headed twelve-year-old who'd arrived two weeks ago, and he was still miserable and homesick. He lay on the floor bawling his lungs out, so I stopped and tried to cheer him up. I told him the Diggers were his new family. We took care of each other. In a month his home would be a dream—like something he'd made up, make-believe. He said he didn't want it to be a dream, he didn't want to forget. I don't know why, but that made me sad.

"Listen," I said. "You're a Digger now. Get used to it. In six or seven years the clay dust will fill your lungs—"

"No," he whined, "Boss Callow gave me a mask!"

"Boss Callow gave us all masks, but they don't do a thing. The clay dust is so fine, there is no way to filter it. That's why the sky is red. That's why Boss Callow stays in the tower and breathes bottled air. That's why nobody but the Diggers remain on Slabour for more than a month at a time. *There is no way to escape it.* The sooner you forget about your home, the sooner you can start living again."

He stopped his bawling. He looked at me with big, blue eyes, red from squeezing.

"You mean I'm gonna die?"

"You'll live to be nineteen or twenty. Possibly twenty-one. But it's all right! It's a short life, but it's a life. And you couldn't want a better family than the Diggers."

"I have a mask—Boss Callow gave me a mask."

Hopeless. I gave up. He'd come around in his own good time. We all had.

Simon and Mo were waiting at the sonic shower. Although it was strictly prohibited, we each put coins in the meter, splitting the cost, and squeezed into the stall together. We knew we'd never save enough to leave, but we all nursed the fantasy. Sometimes you have to, to get through the days.

The scru-shed was a mile from the barracks via a crude path where the clay had been stamped flat by a million Digger boots. There were no porta-walks—in fact, there was nothing on Slabour that wasn't absolutely necessary for keeping us alive and sane and digging. Serendipity Pharmaceuticals wanted the Creelium crystals mined as cheaply as possible, and people did the job cheaper than machines.

We were halfway there when a voice stopped us cold.

"Early for a scru, isn't it?"

We turned around and there was Boss Callow's milky white eye. It was as big as my head and it hovered five feet off the ground. It looked like a real eye, but it was just a machine he worked from his room in the tower, so he could watch us and talk to us without leaving his comfortable lounger. And a mean little stinger was built into the pupil in case we misbehaved.

"We like to go before dinner, sir," Simon said politely. "It's less crowded."

"And you have first pick of the girls, eh?" A metallic membrane passed across the eye, a lewd sort of wink. "I envy you. When I was a lad, I would have given my right hand for ten new girls a month."

"Or ten little boys," I said, under my breath.

Callow picked his favorite from every new shipment of Diggers, dressed him in lace, and put him to work as his handservant. Once upon a time he had picked me.

"What?" asked the eye.

"Nothing," I said.

"Nothing . . . ?"

"Nothing, sir."

"That's better."

"Carnal delights," the eye mused, "pleasures of the flesh. Ah yes, it's a short life but a sweet one. By the time you boys are twenty you'll have scrued more girls than most men do in a lifetime."

"If we live that long," I said.

Nobody ever talked back to Collow for fear of his sting. I couldn't understand what had come over me. I suppose it was the little boy Sennel, thinking Callow had done him such a favor with the worthless mask.

The eye floated over to my face, so close I could hear the machinery whirring inside.

"I don't like that tone of voice."

"Then why don't you come out of your tower," I said, "and do something about it instead of hiding behind the eye—"

"I will not tolerate disrespect!"

"And I will not tolerate . . ." What was I saying? I couldn't stop myself.

"I will not tolerate you—you lying cowardly bag of borselshit!"

The next thing I knew I was lying in a clay pit ten feet off the road. I'd been stung before—I knew the sensations, the pounding in my head, the feeling that my rear teeth were biting metal. Simon and Mo were trying to help me stand, but my legs were twitching uncontrollably.

Boss Callow's eye was gone.

3

They eased me onto the floor and dripped lixor down my throat until the pain had dulled. I stared at a vu-screen—the only furnishing—where women were performing sexual acts with men, women, children, animals, and robots, alone and in groups. It was supposed to be exciting, but, because I'd seen it so many times before, the effect was the opposite, calming, hypnotic.

"That bastard," Simon was saying. "I'd like to rub clay in his eye."

"Drag him out of the tower," Mo agreed, "stamp his ribs in. Drink some more."

He tilted the glass to my lips, poured too fast so I choked and the thick syrup ran down the corner of my mouth. I wiped it away with the back of my hand and lay back and looked over the new girls.

You could always tell the fashion on the big, urban planets by what they were wearing. I remember when it was "The Tumor," a gray sack which covered a girl from head to toe and made bubble-shaped bulges everywhere on her body except where nature intended. Then, some shimmery fabric that clung with electro static glue. They could have painted themselves and saved the money. After that, Fey-bird plumes and hats like dinner plates. Whatever the fashion, rest assured it was the opposite of whatever had come before and totally impractical. The new bunch was wearing short skirts held up by suspenders, kaleidoscope stockings, and knee-high boots.

None of them excited me. But since I'd been through the trouble of getting here, I started toward a plump blond girl.

Simon blocked my path.

"No, she's not for you."

"What do you mean? Since when do you do my choosing?"

"Trust me," he said solemnly.

So I picked a lanky, green-haired girl with almond eyes.

"Nope."

"Simon!" I was getting annoyed. "It just so happens I want that one. I want to scru her."

"You're making a mistake."

"If that doesn't beat all! You talk me into coming here when I'm not in the mood, then you tell me I can't pick my girl. You're asking for a poke, Simon, you really are."

"Calm down. There are girls upstairs still. One might tickle you. All I'm suggesting is you wait and look 'em over. That's all."

Simon sang a song to pass the time. It was one he'd made up and it was my favorite.

> "I'm the blackbird of space,
> Go where I will,
> Fly to the Milky Way,
> Drink my fill,
> Bathe in the stardust
> Till my feathers turn gold,
> Wander the heavens
> Till I'm ninety years old
>
> I'll come of age, for no fool would chase
> Or try to cage the blackbird of space.
> A ripe old age, for no fool would chase
> Or try to cage the blackbird—
>
> The blackbird of space."

The girls kneeled at his feet, listening with their eyes closed. They were star-hoppers and the song meant a lot to them. I could see the weariness, the melancholy on their faces.

Mo broke the silence. He stuck his elbow in my ribs and pointed to the staircase.

"Look at that one! How'd you like to give her a roll?"

The boots, the shifting geometrics of her stockings, the familiar curve of her hips under the skirt. But it was her walk I recognized. A woman's walk is the most distinctive thing about her, more her own than her features or her figure or her DNA print.

She came across the room with an easy sway, stopped in front of me, gazed at me with her soft, sad eyes.

"This spaceman looks familiar. Looks like a boy I once knew. But now he's all grown and sprouting a beard. Are you the same one, spaceman? Do you cheat at speckers?"

I kissed her hair and her eyes and the soft place beneath her jaw.

"Suki, how did you—I thought, I mean I didn't think I'd ever—oh Suki, how did you ever get here?"

She said she'd been stopped over at Romine 3. A shift of Scrugals was waiting to be shipped to Slabour. One went through the Change, so she volunteered to go in her place.

"Suki was down at the mines this morning," Simon said, "looking for you. I promised to bring you by."

"Yeah," Mo said. "We promised."

We went upstairs and I put coins in the meter outside her cubicle. Enough for half an hour—it was all the coins I had. The door slid open and closed behind us and we were alone, except for the damned monitor. There's always *somebody* watching. I started to kiss her and she drew back as if I were trying to feed her a spoon of something awful. She looked nervous, uncomfortable.

"I'd be lying," she said, "if I told you I shipped to this horrible place because I wanted to see you. Oh, I do want to see you—you're very special to me, Stefin, you've stuck in my mind all these years. But I'm tired of lying. I'm tired of pretending that I enjoy the panting, leering scruers, and I'm tired of being bought and sold and shipped from this star system to the next like a piece of machinery."

"I thought you liked being a scrugal," I said. "You always seemed to like it."

"Oh, Stefin." She shook her head. "Remember you told me a story about when you first came to Slabour? Boss Callow picked you for his handservant. You wouldn't have had to work in the mines. You would have stayed in the tower, breathed the bottled air and lived years longer. But you refused to—"

"He wanted me to wear a dress and drink his jism. He wanted to make an animal out of me."

"So now, love, do you understand? What you found intolerable for a day is the constant condition of my life."

"Then why do you do it?"

She picked her toy Kimba bear off the air-cot and regarded it thoughtfully. It was a lucky charm; she always traveled with it, believing it stopped the starships from crashing. Scrugals are awfully superstitious.

"Fear," she said. "I had no skills or education. I had nobody to take care of me. I was terrified of growing old, and I couldn't afford youthification. Scrulux Corporation took care of all that. And they promised me a good pension after the Change. But it's not enough. Better free, Stefin, free and frightened and never knowing what the next day will bring."

She took me by the shoulders and looked into my eyes. Her voice grew deadly earnest.

"I've found a way to buy out of my contract. Help me and I'll help you escape."

"There is no escape from Slabour," I said.

"I think I know of a way. There will be a considerable risk, but you have little to lose."

"What about Arne-Tak?" I whispered. Arne-Tak was the execupimp; he was probably monitoring us at that very moment. "He'll alert Boss Callow and—"

"No, Arne-Tak is a part of it. He wants to buy raw Creelium. He'll pay 50,000 CUs a gram and arrange our escape. Imagine, Stefin! Smuggle a handful of Creelium out of the mines and we'll be free and rich and have the galaxy at our feet."

I shook my head.

"When we come out of the mines we have to pass before a Locator. If there is Creelium anywhere on our bodies, it glows green. Once a Digger I knew arranged to sell Creelium to a shuttle pilot in return for his freedom. He ate it, thinking that the thickness of his body would shield the glow. But when he passed in front of the Locator his whole stomach lighted up green. Know what they did?"

"What?"

"Cut open his stomach. Right there in front of us, they cut open his stomach and picked out the crystals. It wasn't a pleasant sight."

"My plan is better, Stefin. There is still risk—and it will demand a very great sacrifice of you. But the gain will be far greater. Listen closely love, here is what you must do . . ."

4

The artificial sun was dying, the blood sky turning black, as Simon, Mo and I hiked back along the path to the barracks. They were comparing their girls, bragging about their exploits. When Simon asked me why I was so silent, I shook my head, and I was glad when he didn't press me.

Later that night I stopped by Sennel-Rey's hammock. I felt guilty about that afternoon and wanted to reassure him. But he wasn't there.

I asked his neighbor, a boy named Rhone, if he'd seen him.

"Didn't you hear?" Rhone said. "He shipped back home."

That's Digger talk. That's what we say when somebody dies.

"How?"

"He tried to run away. He didn't understand there was no place to run. He went over the horizon, to the dark side. It's too bad."

"Yeah," I said. "Really too bad."

Slabour's artificial atmosphere and sun were contained on the side of the planet where the Diggers lived and mined. At night, when the sun went out, the atmosphere held enough heat to last till morning. But cross the horizon—the line delineating the sun's parabola—to the dark side, and you were in the eternal, icy night of space, where no life can exist for more than a heartbeat.

Back in my hammock I thought about the wispy little boy who had bawled so fiercely that afternoon. I saw him in my mind's eye, crossing the horizon. I saw the cold creep over him. I saw him puzzled, hugging himself for warmth, wondering whether to go back, deciding to go on just a little farther. I saw the cold stop him, turn his skin blue, his lips purple, his breath frost white.

Then the moisture of his body forming a delicate latticework of crystals, a lacy fine ice cocoon. Not even a burial. Boss Callow would leave him standing as a warning to others.

13

Suddenly there was nothing comforting about death. He was lurking outside the barracks, real and tangible as myself, counting my days on his fingers. I knew then I had to survive, I had to chance Suki's plan no matter what the consequences.

5

I shimmied down the tunnel and emerged into the mine pocket, where I could stand if I kept my head bent. Simon—the eldest—went before me, and Mo and two other Diggers followed in order of age, as was the custom.

The first thing we do when we open a pocket is install the Locator and the Pulverizer. The Locator, a little box on a tripod, projects a beam that makes the Creelium glow green through the clay, so we know where to dig for it. The Pulverizer has a hammer which crushes the crystals to powder and mixes it with a thick liquid called Gunk. The purpose of the Gunk is twofold: it dissolves whatever clay may have gotten in, and it serves as a medium. The Gunk is piped to the surface and stored in tanks. When the tanks are full—it takes a week—they are loaded aboard a shuttle and shipped to the big refineries on Romine 3. There it is processed into DHX-119-b, the "Synchronicity" drug.

We'd been working the pocket for some time and the machines were already set up. Simon started the Pulverizer (*blam-blam-blam-blam-blam*—you couldn't talk over the noise of the hammer). He scanned the wall with the Locator and a sprinkling of green glowed through the clay. Sometimes there would be chunks as big as eggs, beautiful hexagonal crystals easy to mine. But when it was like this we had to painstakingly dig out every crumb. In an hour I'd broken two fingernails and collected a handful of crystals, like coarse salt. I started for the Pulverizer.

It's funny about fear. Before, there had been terror in my uncertainty. But now that I had decided on the one—the only—possible course of action, I was no longer afraid. I caught my toe on a ridge of clay and fell. My hand went out in a natural gesture, and I guided it slightly to the left so it came under the Pulverizer's relentless hammer.

I screamed.

6

"There are two possible procedures," the medic said, when I came out of anesthesia. I was lying on an operating table in the infirmary, breathing the sweet bottled air. "We can fit you with a bionic hand, or we can send your DNA print to Sifra-Messa and have them regenerate one. The bionic we do right here—I'll fit it myself. Cost about 800 CUs and you can go back to work immediately. The regenerated one's got to run 5,000, and who knows how much work you'll miss waiting around for it. If I were you I'd go bionic."

He nodded at me, the harsh light overhead glaring off his old-fashioned spectacles. He was balding, pink, dressed in a white smock. He bit at a hangnail while he spoke.

"Bionic hand will do everything your old one did except feel. Regenerated—she'll feel, but I don't think that makes up for the cost and inconvenience. That's my opinion. Ah!"

I guess he got rid of the hangnail. He held up his thumb and admired it.

"What do you say? Bionic or regenerated?"

I hesitated. "Bionic?"

"Good choice. Just what I'd do in your boots."

He measured my right hand with calipers, jotting down numbers on a clipboard. Then he measured the stump of my left hand. Then he went to the storeroom where they kept the cellpastes and the bonestock and bin after bin of bionic limbs in graduated sizes.

I lay waiting, the harsh light filtering orange through my eyelids. Odd, not to have a left hand. Like missing a step in the dark. I could feel my fingers moving, but I couldn't actually feel the fingers. I touched the stump. The wristbones were like pebbles in a sack of skin.

Two hours later I was back in the mines, digging with my new bionic hand. It didn't look anything like the real one; the nails were embossed in the plastic, the skin was a uniform fleshtone—lighter than my own—and the mechanical fingers were ungainly. It didn't work like the real one either; I had trouble coordinating it and of course I couldn't feel the clay.

I waited, and when the other Diggers were occupied I snapped open the wrist. How strange it looked!—a clean, square hole filled with printed circuits, wafer-thin batteries, and the micro-servomechanisms which turned my nerve impulses into finger motions.

Quickly I filled the hole with Creelium crystals and snapped shut the cover.

"Trouble with your new limb, Stefin?"

Boss Callow's eye was hovering behind me. He was always notified of our accidents. But how long had he been there? How much had he seen?

"I was checking the batteries, sir."

"Were you now? Let's have a look at it."

I held up the hand, turned it front and back.

"And where are the batteries?" he asked.

"In this compartment here, sir."

I tapped the wrist, my heart pounding.

"That opens up, does it? Fascinating. You know, you're a lucky lad. In my time, if you lost a limb, well—you lost a limb and that was that. Bionics were prohibitively expensive. DNA engineering and regeneration were still highly experimental. What's it look like on the inside?"

"Sir?"

"Inside the wrist, where the batteries go. Open it up so I can have a look."

"I'm not sure how to do that," I said.

"Nonsense, you had it open when I came in. Don't be troublesome. I was hoping that sting might have taught you a lesson. Won't have to sting you again, will we?"

"No sir."

Slowly I reached for the wrist.

Suddenly the Pulverizer screeched and died, and Simon, who was standing beside it, let out with a string of curses.

The eye floated over to him.

"What's the problem?"

"Seems to have jammed up, sir," Simon said.

The eye observed while we stripped down the Pulverizer and found, wedged between the gears, a coin. Boss Callow got so angry he forgot about my hand. He said that further sabotage of this sort would land us all in the LAS. Laziness would not be tolerated! With that he spun around and sailed away.

We came out of the mines at nightfall and passed before the Locator. I was shaking by the time my turn came—I wanted to give myself up right then and there—but the casing of my bionic hand shielded the Creelium precisely as Suki had planned.

On our way back to the barracks Simon sent Mo ahead to get first dibs on the shower. Then he said to me in a low voice:

"Congratulations. I didn't think you'd pull it off."

"Pull what off?"

"Smuggling Creelium."

"What Creelium? What are you talking about?"

"Don't play stupid with me. I've been a Digger longer than any of you. I thought I knew every trick—but when you dumped those crystals inside your hand, that was a new one. A good one too. Don't act so surprised! Who do you think dropped the coin in the pulverizer?"

I'd never heard Simon like this. There was admiration in his voice, but also envy and anger.

"Simon, if it works—if I get off this asteroid alive—I'll be back for you. I won't forget."

"Borselshit you will."

"No, really."

"Who's buying the crystals? One of the shuttle pilots? Or a Guard? I know, it's Suki—that's why she shipped back. Am I right?"

I was silent.

"Whoever it is," Simon went on, "make sure you can trust them. If you mess this, you'll be in the LAS for a month."

"If it works I'll be back for you, Simon. For you and Mo and all the rest. I promise."

"Borselshit."

I went straight from the barracks to the scru-shed. Alone with Suki in her cubicle, I snapped open the wrist.

She gasped at the sight of so much wealth. She smiled at me—not her sad smile, but a smile false as my new hand. She tried to kiss me and I pushed her away.

"Let's get on with it," I said.

"Don't hate me for this, Stefin."

"I don't hate you—I'm just not in the mood for kissing. What do we do now? How do we . . .?"

The door began to open. Instantly I dumped the crystals into her jewelry box—a hollow pearl as big as a fist—and sealed it before the intruder could see what I was doing.

He was old, scaly skin, squinty eyes, leering lips. Wisps of white floss strayed from his temples, and a blue caftan draped his hobbled form. He was Arne-Tak, the execupimp.

"Where is the Creelium?" he said.

I made sure not to look at the jewelry box (people's eyes often betray their secrets).

"Where is the money?" I demanded. "How will I escape?"

"There is a shuttle leaving at midnight. You will be aboard. The pilot has been paid."

"What about Suki?"

"She'll have her money—when I have my Creelium. Suspicious, aren't you? But it's no matter to me if Callow loses a Digger. Even a fine, handsome one like you."

He squeezed my arm with pincer fingers. I shook him off.

"Gently, please," he said. "I'm an old man with plastic teeth. I'm stuck together with cell paste. In a few years there won't be enough left to patch, and I'll use the profits from this transaction to retire to a green planet where I can die beneath a blue sky. Now hand it over, sweet boy, will you please?"

"Give her the money first."

He flared. "You dare order me around? Why I could—"

But then he cackled and patted my shoulder. "Of course I will."

He peeled a 1,000 CU not from his billfold and handed it to her.

"She'll have the rest when I have the Creelium."

I looked to Suki.

"Give it to him," she said.

"But—"

"Give him the Creelium."

I passed him the jewelry box. He emptied the Creelium into a leather pouch and stashed it in his caftan. He was grinning, and his perfect plastic teeth were like a row of tombstones.

"Wait here," he said. "The pilot will come to get you. Meanwhile, I will pay Suki what she has coming."

He took her slim wrist and pulled her toward the door.

"Suki's staying with me," I said, but I'm afraid it sounded more like a question than a statement of fact.

"She'll be on the shuttle." He grinned. "Don't worry your pretty head."

He pulled her out to the hall, and before I could object the door had closed between us, sealing me in the cubicle. I tried the door, but it wouldn't open. I paced and lay down on the air-cot, my plastic hand an uncomfortable pillow for my head. Then I got up, because the door was opening. Two security guards in black uniforms and black helmets came in and handcuffed me.

8

Boss Callow was plump, all smooth and round as though he'd been blown up with gas. His oiled hair made a row of curls on his forehead, and his face was the face of an arrogant, pudgy child.

He lay on his lounger frowning at me for what seemed like forever after the security guards delivered me. His milky white eye was staring at me too, from a stand at the other side of the room. It was just dead machinery, but it gave me the creeps, having three eyes on me.

At last he said, "I understand you've been smuggling Creelium. Planning escape. Conspiring with Scrugals. What do you have to say for yourself?"

"Nothing, sir."

"Nothing?"

He raised an eyebrow.

A little boy came in with a carafe of lixor and a tray of food. He was tow-headed, frail, dressed in a frilly smock. Reminded me of Sennel-Rey. While he was pouring the lixor, Boss Callow reached out to tousle his hair.

"Know what these are?" Callow said, after the boy had gone.

He picked something off the tray and held it up so I could see. An orange crustacean—or insect, I couldn't be sure—with a pointed head, big scissor legs in back and little ones in front, bound with thread. The animal squirmed in his grasp.

"It's a lobsopper," he said. "A rare delicacy. Imported from Altair 4—or is it 5? No matter. The taste is incomparable. You crack the head between your teeth and suck out the insides."

As he did so the lobsopper let out a high shriek. He tossed aside the empty shell and reached for another, talking while he chewed.

"Don't be shocked, Stefin dear. They don't feel a thing. Very low order of intelligence. But, do you know?—I think if they had human consciousness, they would feel proud to be eaten. On their home planet they hop around doing nothing, helping no one. But when I eat them, they bring me the greatest pleasure and satisfaction. Increase virility too. Ahhh!"

He tossed away another shell and washed it down with lixor.

"Likewise, Stefin, if you hadn't come to Slabour you would be leading a silly, idle existence, wasting your time with this and that. Instead you are performing one of the most vital tasks in the universe, mining Creelium for the Synch drug. Scientists and statesmen and artists depend on it for the accidents which give them inspiration. Why, a lump of Creelium mined with your own two hands might someday stop an intergalactic war, or give a scientist a clue to the secret of immortality. That is why I *cannot* understand your dissatisfaction. Half the beings in the galaxy would give a limb to be in your place doing good, useful work." He paused to crack another head between his teeth. "I hope you will give careful thought to what I've said. Now I'm afraid I must punish you."

He rang for the guards. They came and stood on either side of me.

"Take him to the LAS," Boss Callow said.

9

They led me downstairs, to a bright little room lined with instrument banks. They put me in a chair that was bolted to the floor and exchanged my handcuffs for wrist clamps and ankle clamps and a belt around my chest. My head fitted into a kind of vise and a helmet hung above me. Then the guards stepped back and my old friend the medic came in. He started scraping a small circle in my scalp.

"Nice to see you again," he said cheerfully. Healing or hurting, it didn't seem to make much difference to him.

"Have you been in the LAS before?"

"No."

"LAS stands for Limbic Access Stimulator. The limbic system is located in the deepest part of the cerebral cortex, just above the midline brain. It's the seat of man's primal appetites and emotions. Hunger, sexual desire, pleasure. Fear. Fear's the one we're interested in. We lower the helmet and a filament slips through the skull, right into the fear center. Stimulate the area with an electric current and—bingo! Hold still."

He was tightening the vise around my temples.

"Got to keep the head properly positioned," the medic droned on. "Miss the fear center by a millimeter and we wind up stimulating pleasure or hunger. Say, how's that new hand working out? Glad you went bionic?"

"Yeah." I had a thought. "Do you miss the fear center often?"

"One time out of a hundred. Don't waste your time hoping."

He went to a control panel on the wall and pulled a switch. The helmet slid down over my head. I'd take his word for the filament—I didn't feel a thing.

When I was a child I was scared of the dark. My mother would sit at the edge of my bed and tiptoe away when she thought I'd fallen asleep. And I would lie there with my eyes open, watching for the winged snappersnatch that could fly to my second-story window. Silhouettes of my bedroom furniture threatened to turn into monsters, and if I stared too long at the pile of clothes on the chair, it might rise and come for me, inhabited by a ghostly presence.

But what could scare me now? Not death—we Diggers flirted with death, he was our lover. Nor mutilation, for that too was part of our lives. What then?

I felt uneasy. Still alone with the medic in that bright little room, but now there was a third. Somebody—wait, I knew him! I was an infant in my crib and I knew him. He came whispering, came with a shuffling step, dressed in shadowy robes—*oh god, the Faceless Man, it was the Faceless Man come to take me away in his sack*!

I wanted to scream and scream and never stop, but I didn't. I grinned. Chuckled. Breathing slow, calm. Make it look like I was having the time of my life. Only chance. Hold out a little longer. *Whispering. Closer now. The sack, suffocating.* Couldn't keep it up—crack in a minute, blithering, howling hysteria—

It stopped.

The helmet rose from my head. The medic strolled over.

"Looks like that's the one time in a hundred." he said. "You're incredibly lucky. We must have hit a pleasure center by mistake." He pulled back my hair and examined the scalp. "Yes, uh-huh, we'll just shift the filament a half-millimeter to the left and try again—have to wait a minute, till the cortical excitement dies down."

"Hey," I said, as if the idea had just come to me. "While we're waiting, could you take a look at my hand? I'm having trouble coordinating it. Could some of the linkages be bad?"

"Doubt it. But you might have gotten clay dust in the servos. Let's see."

He opened the clamp that was holding down my left hand. I brought it up fast under his jaw. His head went up, his old-

fashioned spectacles shattered on the floor. He staggered backward and fell over and lay motionless.

I undid the rest of the clamps and started for the door.
Then I hesitated.

Certainly taking pleasure in another's pain is the most terrible sin. Yet I must confess to enjoying what I did next. I
dragged the medic to the chair, fastened him in and clamped
the his head into the vise. I went back to the control panel,
trying to remember which switches he had pulled. I must
have done it right—the helmet slid onto his head and in a
moment he was squirming, mumbling and flinching like a
man in a troubled sleep. His eyes opened. He saw me at the
controls and they opened wider. Then his pupils rolled up so
his eyes were white and he was screaming and drooling. I
would have liked to stay and watch, but the LEDS on the
control panel said 23:43—seventeen minutes to get on the
shuttle.

I ran through the basement of the tower and up the stairs,
my boot heels echoing in the quiet. Carefully now, the entrance was around the corner and a guard would be on duty.

I meant to plan a strategy, but the sight of him—he was
one of the guards who's taken me to see Callow—filled me
with such rage that I rushed him head on. He didn't even go
for his stinger, he was so surprised. He covered his face with
his arms and lowered his head so the helmet would protect
him, I hit him in the stomach with my hard plastic hand; he
doubled over on the floor and I kicked him. I must have been
crazy—I wanted to kill him. I grabbed his stinger off the
floor and jammed the muzzle into his face and pulled the
trigger. Nothing happened. One of the little buttons on the
stock must have been a safety device, but I didn't have time
to figure it out now. I swung it around and smacked him in
the head with the butt. Then I put the stinger under my arm
and started running.

Eight, nine minutes left. The hard path hurt my knees. The
stinger was jiggling, making a sore spot under my arm, and
the dust in my lungs left me gasping.

The Scrulux shuttle was a small, snub-nosed ship with
stubby wings for atmospheric flight. It lay in the middle of a
broad, floodlighted bowl, surrounded by an electric fence. I
waited by the gate, huddled in the shadows while two guards
cleared the area in preparation for liftoff. The shuttle hatch, I
was relieved to see, was still open.

When the guards came out of the gate I slipped inside. I'm

pretty small and fast on my feet. I guess they didn't notice me, because they closed the gate and strolled away, chatting about how they were going to spend their vacation hunting 'barians on some planet called Junglabesh.

Crouching, I scurried across the bowl. Then up the gangplank and into the ship. Two rows of five seats, an aisle down the middle. Ten very surprised Scrugals.

Suki climbed out of her seat and ran up to me.

"Stefin—"

"You set me up. I loved you and I trusted you and you set me up for the LAS!"

"No, no I didn't. It was Arne-Tak; please believe me! I thought we'd escape together. I didn't know he'd betray us— yes, *us*, Stefin, he cheated me too—kept all the Creelium and wouldn't give me money. Now I'll never buy back my contract, I'll be a Scrugal forever."

The *FASTEN HARNESS* sign went on and the girls began buckling themselves in.

"I lost my hand for you," I said. "I've got to live the rest of my life with this machine at the end of my arm."

"Stefin, I'm sorry, I'm sorry, I never thought it would end like this."

The plump blond Scrugal called to her, "Suki, you'd better get in your lounger, we're lifting off."

Both of us looked down the cabin. Ten loungers, air for ten, food for ten. The tiny ship would carry ten passengers and no more.

The pilot's voice came over the intercom:

"All ready, girls? Seat four's not buckled. Buckle up, seat four, I'm closing the hatch."

That was Suki's seat.

The hatch began to slide shut.

"Stefin," Suki whispered, "Go in my place."

"No."

"You've got to—if they find you now they'll kill you."

"But—what about you?"

"Don't worry, I'm safe. Goodbye, love."

"*No!*" I screamed. "*Suki!*"

The hatch was almost closed, but she slipped out. I grabbed the edge with my fingertips and tried to pull it open. I hammered on the hatch with my fists.

The pilot's voice again:

"Seat four, you're still not buckled. Can't wait any longer— we'll miss perihelion."

I stood there dazed as the ship came to life, the hiss of the cabin being pressurized, the rumble of the compressor, the chugging fuel pumps.

The plump blond girl undid her harness. She pulled me back to the seat next to her and buckled me in.

"Suki can take care of herself," she said. "She'll be all right. Now lie back and relax—it's easier to take the acceleration. That's right, good. Deep breaths."

I felt a lump under my hip. I squirmed around and reached down. There, tucked under the cushion, was the toy Kimba bear, Suki's good-luck charm. I dug my fingers into the fur as the ship began to move.

10

The shuttle pilot—Bonner-Di was the name on his breast pocket—had a crew-cut and a square jaw and cool blue eyes that hardly flickered when he found me sitting in the seat where Suki should have been. I'd passed out during acceleration, letting the stinger slip to the floor, and now he was holding it, pointing the muzzle at me. I followed his orders and walked in front of him to the cockpit, my hands in the air.

The co-pilot, a younger man, was watching data flow across a vu-screen when we entered. Bonner-Di ordered him to the back of the ship to double-check some apparatus. Then we were alone and he put down the stinger and grinned at me.

"I'm always hoping one of you kids will sneak on board, get away from that damn awful place. I have a boy your age, and the thought of him getting tricked into one of those mining contracts makes my blood run cold. Bad enough he can't be here with me. Oh, I guess he could, but he's better off on Sirus. I've got an apartment on Romine 3 for when I'm not flying, but I wouldn't want a kid to grow up there. With all the refineries and the smoke, it's almost as bad as Slabour. So

I got him and his ma a ranch on Sirus, all meadows and trees and flowers. He's even got his own borsel to ride! I gave it to him for his fifteenth birthday. I see them two, three times a year. Five more years flying the shuttle for Scrulux and my contract's up. I'll move to Sirus and be with them year round. God, I miss them."

He'd grown warm and animated recalling his family. He turned serious again when one of the instruments went *beep-beep-beep*. He pressed a button and a voice crackled into the cockpit:

"Come in Scrulux shuttle B. This is Serendipity, Slabour mining camp. Urgent."

Bonner shot me a look. He adjusted the microphone around his neck, pressed another button and said, "Scrulux shuttle B. What can I do for you, Slabour mining?"

"We have a fugitive Digger, possibly stowawayed on your ship. Stefin-Dae, seventeen, five foot six, 121 pounds standard, complexion light, hair blonde curly, eyes hazel, distinguishing features bionic left hand. DNA print available for confirmation."

"I'll keep an eye out," Bonner said.

"Thanks Scrulux shuttle, good trip."

Bonner switched off communications and frowned at me.

"Tomorrow we'll be docking on Romine 3. Serendipity owns the planet. You won't get ten feet off the shuttle before the security guards spot you and close in."

He squinted at me and scratched his chin, like a tailor sizing me up for a pressure suit. Then he punched some symbols on a keyboard and one of the vu-screens answered with figures that didn't make much sense to me.

Bonner nodded with satisfaction.

"Just what I was hoping. We'll play a little game now, to fool my co-pilot and save my neck. Anyone finds out I willingly aided a fugitive and I'll be in a hell of a fix—lose my pension, maybe my job."

A minute later I pushed Bonner-Di into the passenger cabin, holding the stinger to his neck as though I'd overpowered him. The co-pilot, who was coming up from the rear of the ship, went pale when he saw us. His legs buckled and he grabbed at the handrail for support. I moved down the aisle, keeping Bonner-Di in front of me, warning everybody to stay put or I'd kill him. Truth was I still hadn't figured out how to work the stinger.

The two life rafts in the rear of the shuttle looked like

closets with padded interiors. I backed into one and strapped myself into the harness. For a moment I held the stinger on them—the Scrugals, the co-pilot, Bonner-Di, all watching me as if I were about to do a magic trick—then I tossed it into the aisle. I took a deep breath and grabbed the raft hatch handles and yanked. The hatch snapped shut. The next instant I was slammed back against the padding. The raft had been jettisoned.

I could feel no movement, but I knew I was drifting, drifting with only five inches of metal and insulation and life-sustaining machinery separating me from the annihilating night of space.

Alone in my metal coffin with room enough to raise my head and look at my toes—Digger boots, still dust red. Room enough to reach to the compartment on my left and activate the transmitter that would bleep a distress signal across all navigational frequencies. Room enough to reach the compartment on my right where a week's rations were stored. Room enough to squirm onto my stomach to use the chemical toilet that purified and recycled my wastes. Room for little else.

How long I drifted I cannot say. I tried to mark the plastic harness strap with my fingernail for every passing day—the lights switched on and off to maintain my circadian rhythms —but I soon lost track. Deprived of external stimuli, my dreams grew more and more vivid, invading my waking hours.

I remember one dream, a dream of prisons. I would ingeniously escape only to find myself in another more impossible one. There were thousands and thousands of them, and when finally I imagined I had escaped them all, I found that I myself was a prison, my conditioning, my mortality from which there was no escape.

A time came when I struggled out of my dreams to reach in the compartment on my right for a nutra-bar. I felt all around it, I felt in every corner. I even wriggled into a position where I could peer inside by the pale raft light.

Empty.

I felt a great calm. I had done the impossible, escaped from Slabour. One can die well having done the impossible.

Part II

The Brave 'Barian Hunter

One lie
Begets another.
They gather like the threads
Of the hangman's rope.
   —The Holy Tapes of Bode-Satva
      (Tape #42,100)

1

A finger pulled back my eyelid. Faces, grotesquely large, filling my vision, and concerned voices, all dim and disjointed. Then flat on my back being rolled down a corridor. Needles pricking my flesh, bright light in my eyes, tubes forced down my throat. Later, lying in a lounger—Boss Callow's eye! No, it was a sun in the sky.

I was alive, that much I knew, but my consciousness was a shattered lens. I tried to gather the pieces, a piece of sun in the sky, a piece of blue lake and splashing swimmers, a piece of freckled face. Flowers—I remembered them from home—and an arbor and a flock of lambits. A soft robe (where were my coveralls?) and somebody spooning me hot soup. I had to reconstruct the lens, but the pieces didn't fit. This serious freckled face, she could probably explain if I asked.

"You are," she replied, speaking slowly so I could consider every word, "on the luxury cruiser *Maya*. This is the solarium. "You've been very, very sick. Do you understand?"

I nodded. "I was starving to death."

She smiled despite herself.

"Not exactly. I imagine you were in a sensory-deprivation delirium. You didn't touch the rations—you ate the transmitter."

"I . . . I ate the transmitter?"

"I spent two hours picking chewed microcircuits out of your stomach. I've never performed an operation like it."

Vaguely I remembered:

Compartment on my left, activate the transmitter. Compartment on my right where rations were stored.

My head had been so fogged, so full of noble thoughts of death, that I hadn't remembered my right from my left. Those little square transmitter modules—no wonder they were so hard to swallow!

"What is your name?" she said slowly. I had the feeling

31

this was part of a test to see if my brain was working properly.

I started to answer. Then it occurred to me that I was still a fugitive. I would do well to lie, but the lie would have to be carefully thought out. So I shrugged and looked stupid, which Simon used to tell me was something I did pretty well.

"Where are you from?"

Another shrug.

"You were on a liferaft. Your ship must have been wrecked. *Try* to remember."

I felt awful disappointing her. She was so pretty, kneeling next to my lounger, so serious and intense. Her eyes were blue with long pale lashes. The skin around them showed a fine network of wrinkles which deepened when she smiled. Her ash-blond hair was pulled back and tied with a ribbon. Her white medic's robe was open at the neck—when she leaned forward I could see the swell of her breasts. She saw where I was looking and smiled.

"I think you're getting your health back. We'll take you to the captain in a day or two and see what he wants to do with you."

I guess I looked scared. She rubbed my shoulder and told me not to worry.

"He's a generous man. He'll assign you a job to work off your passage."

Now I was scared. That had an unpleasantly familiar ring to it. Of course they didn't have Creelium mines on luxury cruisers, but they probably had engine rooms, hellishly hot places where I might be shoveling fuel till I drowned in my own sweat.

"You do have to work," she said sympathetically. "Everybody has to work. You can't just lie around in the sun all day unless you're terribly rich."

She gazed across the meadow at some passengers reclining under an arbor. They wore brightly colored robes embroidered with metallic threads, and lots of heavy jewelry. They were eating a nine-course picnic lunch as if it might be their last.

Her voice dropped to a whisper:

"Hypochondriacs, every one of them. They all want to have exotic diseases and a hundred and one pills to take." She sighed. "All my medical training—and here I am passing out placebos. Well, that's my problem. Close your eyes now, try and get some sleep."

I lay on my lounger for the rest of the afternoon, watching the passengers amble across the meadow and play with the lambits, watching them shed their robes by the lakeside for a swim. I could hardly believe I was inside a ship. But squinting, I could discern the far wall of the solarium dome, painted to give the impression of endless meadow. I closed my eyes and felt the sun baking me whole again.

A movement awoke me. A steward was guiding my lounger out of the solarium. It must have been equipped with an air-cushion, for it slid across the grass like a whisper.

A porta-walk sped us down a narrow corridor, and into another dome, this one laid out like a small city with shops and parks and eateries of every planetary cuisine. There were street lamps, trees and shrubbery, and clever lighting to make it seem like an outdoor evening. The most beautiful women strutted past me, and men so fat and fine, so carefully curried that I had to wonder if they were a different species from myself.

The sight of so many people excited me. It was as though I had lived on bread and water, and suddenly a banquet was laid before me, subtle sweets and bitters, every sort of saltiness. I wanted to leap from my lounger and gobble it up until my belly burst with new experiences.

But what if the captain were to put me to work in the bowels of the ship and never let me venture to the upper levels? How awful that would be! When time came for our meeting I would have to impress him as a *very* special person indeed, one who could not possibly be denigrated to working in an engine room.

A porta-walk carried us through another tube, and I began to get a picture of the ship in my mind. Spheres of varying dimension connected by passage tubes—it must have looked like the models of molecules we studied in school, only incredibly vast.

Now we were passing down a corridor less elegant than the rest, plastic treads instead of carpeting, bare metal walls instead of the lavish tapestries hung elsewhere. Probably the crew's quarters.

The steward flashed a light key at one of the doors and slid me inside. The cubicle had a hammock, a chair, a desk, a vu-screen terminal, a sink and a toilet and a smell of disinfectant. Austere, but sheer luxury after the Diggers' barracks. He helped me to the hammock, told me to press the blue button if I felt any pain, and left.

I walked around a little, opening drawers and closets, flushing the toilet. Then I got back on the hammock and settled down to the serious business of making up an identity. They knew I'd been on a liferaft, so I started there and worked backward. I'd say my ship had been wrecked. But where was it going? Why was I aboard?

I knew of three inhabited worlds in this star system. Slabour and Romine 3 were out, for obvious reasons. I'd overheard security guards planning a journey to Junglabesh, to hunt Junglabarians—whatever they were. Yes, that was good. I'd say I was aboard a safari ship bound for Junglabesh. In fact . . . I was the guide! That had an impressive ring to it. Then a meteor had punctured the hull and the crew was sucked out by the vacuum, like the pulp from a lobsopper. I alone reached the liferaft. I alone escaped. Yes, that sounded reasonable. Sort of.

2

"I know who I am," I told my medic next day in the solarium.

She kneeled next to my lounger, listening intently, nodding encouragement. When I came to "safari ship bound for Junglabesh" she drew in her breath sharply.

"But, you're so young—how could they expose you to the danger?"

I chuckled as though danger were my daily fare. "Once you understand the Junglabarians, it's like bagging Kimbas."

"That's not what I've heard. You must be a remarkable young man."

"Well . . . no, not really."

"And awfully modest."

I guessed I'd made the desired impression.

"I'd better go tell the captain," she continued.

"What about me?"

"I think you can walk around now. But don't overdo it. And be in bed by 21:00 sharp—promise?"

Smiling, she straightened the collar of my robe. Something about me brings out the mother in women.

I was windowshopping in the main sphere about two hours later when a steward approached me. He was the same fellow who'd shown me to my room the day before, but you'd never have known it from his manner. Yesterday he was a picture of indifference. Now he was bowing and scraping and with a little urging might have kissed my toes.

"Please let me apologize for last night—that was our only free room. Now we have another vacancy that may be more to your liking. If you'll follow me . . ."

So I followed him through a different sequence of tubes, wondering how a room suddenly becomes vacated on a ship in the middle of deep space, where it's rather hard to get off. Well, maybe somebody died. Or maybe hunters are treated with a little more courtesy than no-account castaways.

"I think you'll find this comfortable," he said, opening a door.

I thought so too. There was room enough for twenty. The walls were gleaming chromium molded in organic curves, the floor, a lamination of colored plastic ribbons. Animal pelts of rich red and green were spread about like puddles of luxury. The furnishings were fabulous affairs of chrome and polished wood and the softest leathers. A vase of flowers and a bowl of fruit sat on a table carved from a cross-section of tree trunk. After a little more bowing and scraping, the steward left and I had a look at the notes attached.

The one with the flowers read, *Honored to have a hunter aboard! Compliments of the Social Director*. And the one with the fruit: *Thrilled to have a hunter with us! Compliments of the Purser*.

Obviously word had gotten around. I bit into a brinko fruit, so ripe the juice ran down my chin, and congratulated myself for foresight and cleverness.

Tomorrow passengers would be asking about my adventures with the Junglabarians. I should know *something* about the savage creatures—at least what they looked like. So I sat down at the entertainment console and requested a vu-screen. It appeared from behind a section of sliding wall. I requested encyclopedic function and in a couple of seconds the screen printed:

ENCYCLOPEDIC FUNCTION
REQUEST TOPIC

"Junglabesh and the Junglabarians," I said.
The screen printed:

REQUEST *ONE* TOPIC

"Junglabarians," I said.

JUNGLABARIANS:
SEE JUNGLABESH

"Terrific," I said. "Allright, Junglabesh."

JUNGLABESH
SECTOR GAMMA 329/969-C
PLANETARY TYPE W-12
ATMOSPHERE ML-6 TRACE
KRYPT ARG HEL NIT . . .

And so forth and so on for the next five minutes. All those
numbers and letters must have meant something to somebody—they sure didn't mean anything to me. I was giving up
hope when the screen cleared and showed me a puffy white
planet set against a starry sky. Some dull music came on,
then a baritone voice:

"'Junglabesh, planet of adventure! Few dare her dense cloud
cover to hunt the savage Junglabarians—fewer still survive to
tell the tale! Yes, for those who love the knife's edge of jeopardy, who shun the security of thirtieth-century life and long
to pit themselves against nature's most vicious manifestation,
no place in the galaxy can compare. Whether your hunting
party decides to float down the Spasa-bam-bam—Junglabesh's
longest river—or hunt on foot through the vast plains of
fleeza, the most common flora, a tall succulent with spade
shaped leaves, you will be guaranteed *the adventure of a lifetime*!

"Now, you are probably wondering about the Junglabarians themselves. How big are they? How fast can they run?
Do you dare engage in hand-to-hand combat with the creatures, or are you better off with a long-distance weapon? The
truth of the matter is—"

The door chime rang.

"Cancel," I said and the screen went blank. I couldn't be
found viewing a primer on a planet I was supposed to know
as well as my own name.

The door slid open.

She smiled slyly as she slipped out of her Scrugal costume, and then she was naked. Except for contragravitational underwear which raised the polar caps of her twin planets to heaven and made them bobble sweetly, when she curtsied.

"Delighted to have a hunter along for the voyage! Compliments of the captain."

3

Among the honors heaped upon me now that I was a hunter was an invitation to dine at the captain's table, delivered via vu-screen next morning. I was to be at the Scandium 5 Eatery at 20:00 sharp. But the Scrugal kept at her work most of the night, and a "quick nap" afterward turned into a whole day's sleep. When I awoke it was nearly 20:30—I passed through the shower, tossed on a robe and ran.

I hoped to find the meal in progress, the captain surrounded by a crowd of drunken boisterous passengers, so I might sneak to my place unnoticed. No such luck.

The maitre d' led me to a dark room decorated with corroded battle axes, shields and spears and suits of armor (the Scandiums had been a race of fierce warriors and terrible cooks—two factors which bring civilization to a rapid end). The captain, the first mate, the purser and five passengers sat around the empty table, fidgeting. They hadn't even ordered yet. They were waiting for me!

"I'm terribly sorry . . ." I began.

The men stood up. The captain beamed.

"Stefin, how good of you to join us."

He was fiftyish, tall and clean-cut. He radiated competency, but his excessive charm made me uneasy. After introductions he sat me at the head of the table opposite him.

"So you're the hunter."

That was a passenger named Olin-Jay who shaved his head and had a lot of muscle turning to fat. His manner was self-consciously crude, as though he were afraid we'd think him a woman if he didn't yawn and belch and pick his nose over dinner.

"That's right," I said pleasantly.

He snorted and shook his head. His wife put it a little more politely.

"Aren't you awfully young?"

"Well ... my dad was a hunter. Probably the greatest hunter who ever lived. And, uh . . . He'd take me hunting with him when I was little. He'd carry me on his shoulders."

I looked around. Nobody was smirking, so I continued, feeling a little safer with my terrain.

"We had some bad times. Once we were traveling down the Sausa-Bam-Bam—that's the longest river on Junglabesh—and a bunch of Junglabarians burst through the fleeza. There were hundreds of them! Junglabarians to my left! Junglabarians to my right! I was ten, I'd never worked a blaster before. But my dad shoved one into my hands. He said, "Son, today's the day you must prove yourself. Without your help, we're finished.' I started blasting away. The Junglabarians were swimming up to our boat and climbing over the side. Too close to blast—I had to beat them away with the butt."

"Don't Junglabarians hate water?"

That was a tall stringy woman with green hair, the wife of a corporate head. Rita-Ploodle, I think was her name.

"Yes, they do! *Usually*. But in cases of all-out battle, nothing stops them."

"Weren't they shooting delirium darts?" Olin-Jay asked, inspecting something he'd removed from his nose.

"As a matter of fact, they were. One of our party was hit in the leg—and he turned on us. We had to knock him unconscious and tie him up with—"

"Yeah," Olin-Jay interrupted. "But how'd you protect yourself from the darts?"

"Oh, the usual ways."

"Did you use umbrella shields?" the corporate head asked. He was Jomama-Ploodle, a prim little man who wiped his mouth with a silk hanky after every bite. "Or magnetic deflectors?"

"Hard to remember—— I think we used umbrella shields."

He nodded approval. His head was almost round, and he plastered down his hair so his ears stuck out like stabilizing fins.

"Then," I continued, "there was the time I lost my hand . . ."

They listened enraptured until the food came, loaves of ground krombar, heavily spiced, drenched in sauce; pâté of snat's heart; and an assortment of native breads, vegetables and condiments. It all might have been made from the same stuff as the spears and battle axes. Three or four bites and I was full. But the rest of them kept eating and eating as if they had digestive bypasses.

After dessert—a sweet pudding of such weight that it threatened to bend my fork—the purser cleared his throat.

"Stefin-Dae, we would like to ask a very great favor."

He was chubby, balding and overly jolly, with tiny eyes. His speech was stilted, as though he'd been rehearsing for hours.

"Our ship is one day's distance from Junglabesh. Olin-Jay and Jomama-Ploodle and some of the other passengers have asked if we might reroute and orbit there, while they shuttle to the surface to hunt Junglabarians. Initially the captain refused because we had no trained hunter to lead the expedition. But now that you are here ..." He cleared his throat again.

"I'm afaid I couldn't possibly," I said quickly. "I've sworn off hunting forever. I took it as an omen, when that meteor wrecked our safari ship. We hunters are a superstitious lot, you know."

Now the captain spoke.

"You realize, Stefin-Dae, that by the laws of space a rescued man must pay prorated passage. We won't be reaching a civilized planet for three months. At that time you will owe us—do you have the figures, Rob-Ti?"

The first mate, a junior version of the captain, flipped through his note-pad.

"389,768 CUs."

"That," the captain said, "is the amount we will credit you for leading a hunting party."

Olin-Jay leaned back in his chair, expanding his stomach as though it were some wonderful accomplishment, and belched.

"I'll throw in another 100,000 for every Junglabarian scalp I bring back."

"I'll match the offer," Jomama-Ploodle said, delicately wiping his fingers.

"Otherwise," the captain said, "I will have to assign you some job aboard ship. I suppose you might qualify for a steward. If so—how long would it take him to work off passage?"

The first mate consulted his notepad.

"A little over eleven years."

"Will you reconsider?" the purser asked me.

4

Alone in my room I reran the tape on Junglabesh. I waited anxiously through the five minutes of statistics, then the dull music and the baritone voice with its pear-shaped tones:

"Now you are probably wondering about the Junglabarians themselves. How big are they? How fast can they run? Do you dare engage in hand-to-hand combat with the creatures, or are you better off with a long-distance weapon? The truth of the matter is, nobody knows! Junglabesh's cloud over is impenetrable! Radiations in this sector of the galaxy make radio transmission impossible! Robot zoological probes are useless!

"Surely hunters have returned from this planet of mystery, you say. Indeed they have!—but so traumatized with fear that no two survivors seem to be able to agree on a description of the 'barians. Some have even returned without seeing any 'barians at all! And doesn't this aura of mystery make the adventure all the more exciting?"

No, I honestly didn't think so. It would have been exciting enough for me to know where and when they slept so I might creep up behind them and knock their brains out.

5

Cagily I cross-examined Olin-Jay, Jomama-Ploodle and Dix-Baedle, a whiny young man who would also be on our hunt. They too seemed confused about whether 'barians were hydrophobic or amphibian, mammalian or reptilian, bipedular or multi-tentacled, pink, green, purple or chartreuse. But they all agreed that the creatures were swift, cunning and vicious. I was careful to flaunt the few facts I'd gleaned from the encyclopedic tape to maintain my aura of expertise. What is an expert, anyway? Only a fellow who knows one more fact than the rest.

6

The four of us went to the firearm shop and browsed through rows of weapons, discussing the merits of this blaster, the disadvantages of that stinger. We settled on heavyweight shockers with infrared homers. They aimed automatically at anything warm. All you had to do was pull the trigger. Blam. Jomama-Ploodle, who seemed to have a conscience about such things, wondered if they were sportsmanlike. I said yes, by all means, the height of sportsmanship. Frankly I would have preferred the heavyweight blaster the shopkeeper claimed could knock a moon out of orbit. But it was so cumbersome I feared it might hinder me when I turned to flee.

We bought knives, binoculars, canteens, nutra-bars, medic kits and a million other dandy gadgets. In another shop we took out special-risk life insurance.

7

The shuttles were housed in a cavernous dome at a far end of the ship, nineteen of them in berths, their smooth shapes dazzling in the arclight. One shuttle had been lowered to a track that terminated at a giant double hatch in the far wall. The smaller hatch of the shuttle was open, and I supervised three stewards who were loading in our shockers and heavy supplies.

Pretty soon the rest of my party arrived with a crowd of wives, mistresses, friends and well-wishers, wearing yellow jumpsuits for camouflage in the fleeza and carrying so many accessories strapped to their bodies and slung over their shoulders, it was a wonder they could stand. Jomama-Ploodle's wife gave him a pair of panties for luck. Olin-Jay was telling his not to worry—and reminding her of the locations of wills, deeds, stocks, bonds and bankbooks. And Dix-Baedle's pretty young mate clung to him so fiercely they had to pry her away when time came to clear the area.

8

After liftoff we unstrapped our harnessess and floated to the rear of the cabin, where the standard seats had been replaced by a casual arrangement of loungers and low tables.

Dix-Baedle passed around a flask of lixor and talked about how happy he was to get away from his newly eterna-wed wife. He was in his twenties, a pasty redhead with a whining voice. His in-laws had given them the cruise for a wedding present, but the liner, large as it was, was proving too small a confinement for the two of them.

Olin-Jay squeezed the flask down his gullet. None of that eternal union for him. He said that sequential monogamy was the only way a man could be happy. New wife every three or four years. Keeps 'em on their toes.

Not in Jomama-Ploodle's opinion. He'd been cohabiting with the same woman twenty-nine years, no complaints. He sipped the lixor and dabbed at the corners of his mouth with a silk hanky. And by the by, all this reminded him of the most hilarious Scrugal story. Purser told it to him just the other day. It seems that two spacemen decided to go to a scru-shed for a night's pleasure—but what the Scrugal didn't know was that one of them had a bionic penis with an on-off switch located in his . . .

I couldn't believe it! In a few hours we would be face to face with the 'barians—and here we were having a party! Were they mad? Or simply too stupid to fear for their lives? I suggested we check our gear. I urged we plan a strategy. I hinted this might not be the ideal time to get numbed on lixor. Olin-Jay told me to stuff it and began a story concerning two robots who wanted to have a baby.

When the pilot announced landing, they were so numb they could barely stagger back to their seats to buckle in. The retrorockets screamed, the landing skids screeched, and we were settled on solid ground.

The hatch slid open and a blast of hot dry air struck my face. The rest of them crowded behind me for a look—I could smell their lixor breath. I squinted against the sunlight, and what I saw was a desolate plain of the palest ocher rushing to meet a fierce white sky. Only the fleeza for relief, like the hands of drowning men reaching for help. I was overwhelmed by the alienness of it.

The terrain offered no refuge; once we left the ship we would be easy targets. Yet this also worked in our favor, since the 'barians had no place to hide. I could see for miles. I would be able to see them coming in time to retreat to the ship, possibly in time to claim a scalp or two.

Presently I shouldered my shocker and skipped down the few steps to the surface. The earth felt good under my feet despite my trepidations.

"Come on," I called, and waved them forward like a general into battle.

"So long," said Dix-Baedle.

"Good luck," said Olin-Jay.

"Get lots of scalps," Jomama-Ploodle advised. "If you're not back in twenty-four hours we're leaving without you."

The hatch slid over their cheerful faces.

"Wait a minute—" I said foolishly. The hatch slammed shut as a scalpel severs the umbilical.

Ah-ha. Now I understood. They were neither mad nor stupid. Actually, they were quite intelligent. They would wait in the safety of the shuttle, drinking, joking and making up lies to tell when they returned to the ship. If I succeeded in bringing back a few scalps, then there would be stories about our incredible cunning. If I didn't come back at all, the stories would be about the cunning of the 'barians.

I heartily wished the three of them impotent, bankrupt and infested with the smallest and stubbornest of space lice.

I turned the selector switch on the infrared homer mounted on the shocker, so it would signal at the movement of anything warm. Then cautiously I began to move away from the ship, keeping my eyes peeled on the horizon, sweeping my shocker from side to side.

I came upon a clump of fleeza. The spade-shaped leaves were swollen like bladders and covered with a fine fur. Seven roots grew from the base, slick and scaly and thick as a man's thigh. They turned and twisted across the parched soil, seeking out moisture. Something about them made my stomach turn—they seemed like entrails laid bare.

I continued on my way. The ground was resolute under my stiff new hiking boots. The sun baked my forehead and my nose. I should have brought a hat.

When the ship was no larger than a silver syringe, I stopped and turned a full circle. For a moment I imagined I was standing on a giant's balding dome. A funny monster he would have been, with his little tufts of fleeza hair. The infrared homer registered nothing. No 'barians in sight—no structure, no artifacts. Aside from some tiny, shiny-shelled creatures which scurried away from my step, nothing moved except the shimmering heat, like imperfections in a lens. I might have been walking through a picture.

I went on, more at ease. The land became hilly, the fleeza closer together. Flying insects appeared, their trembling membranous wings nearly a foot across. They went after the sweat running down my face. I brushed them aside easily.

I slung my shocker over my shoulder so I would have my hands free to climb a steep ridge. At the top I sat down to rest. I took a drink from my canteen and ate a nutra-bar. Another vast plain of fleeza—a forest of it— spread out below me, and beyond that a range of jagged mountains veiled by distance. Still no sign of anything resembling a 'barian.

Suppose—suppose the Junglabarians didn't exist, I thought. Suppose they were a myth propagated by a profession of hunters so that they might earn an easy wage with no skill or risk—except the skill of spinning a good yarn and the risk of being discovered. The more I considered this idea, the more certain I became that it was in fact the case. What a fine, ironic bit of justice! Upon my return I would lie to the men in the shuttle, just as they would lie to their friends aboard the liner.

Now, if I were *really* clever, I would return with a hundred or so "Junglabarian scalps" and collect enough money to live like a rich man. What was a 'barian scalp? Anything I could find that might look like one.

With this aim in mind I clambered down the other side of the ridge and continued my hike. In places the fleeza grew so closely together I had to step between the slick, scaly roots. Presently I came to a clearing. Here was something interesting, a new form of plant life, a patch of colorful melons. Each had a covering of long hairs—black, brown, gray, yellow—and each drooped on a short pinkish stem. Perhaps I could carve one up to look like a 'barian scalp. Worth a try.

I took a knife out of my satchel and grasped a handful of the hairs, so I might raise the melon and take a clean cut at the stem. I gasped; my heart turned to ice. For under the hair was a face.

I fell to my knees for a closer look. It was a head with a heavily bearded face, leathery amber skin. The eyes were closed, the features calm and—yes, yes it was!—it was breathing, very slowly but definitely breathing. I tapped its cheek. The head bobbed and moaned softly. I gave it a soft slap and the eyes popped open. It worked its mouth desperately, trying to find a voice.

"Go—go away. They—they use us for *hands*."

It started to say something else, but then the eyes closed and the head slumped forward.

For five heartbeats I knelt there motionless. Then I jumped to my feet and I started to run. I ran for the shuttle, stretching my legs for every inch of distance, straining my body for every ounce of speed. Rivers of sweat welling under my arms. A stitch in my stomach, a rasp in my throat, gasping for air to feed my desperate lungs. Coming to where the fleeza grew thick, leaping between the roots, pumping my arms—watch it!—broke off a leaf, oozing sap, yellow sap, no matter. What's that behind me? Dare to turn around—oh God, oh God, the roots coming off the fleeza. Not roots at all, they're *snakes*! Squirming after me, everywhere, they're everywhere. Where to run? What to do? Oh God, please save me from them, someone save me. They're on my legs and I'm falling, falling. On my back and they're swarming over me, crawling inside my clothes, wet snakes on my skin, fangs drip and glisten—poison? Oh please, yes, poison and make a quick end of it, take me out of this hell, let me die once and for all and forever, for I can't stand any more, I really can't stand any more, I can't—

Part III

The Golden Ropes of Power

1

Sleep. Like a deep hole. Struggling out of it, climbing the crumbling walls till I saw the daylight of consciousness, then slipping back again, With superhuman effort I woke myself and forced open my eyes. I was buried alive. Only my head emerged from the soil—my naked body was imprisoned in the ground. I couldn't say how long I'd been buried, but I could feel sunburn blisters on my nose and forehead. All around me heads drooped on thick pink stems. And I had thought them to be melons! How many years had they been buried for their hair to grow so long?

The ground shook. I could tilt my head back just far enough to see our shuttle ship raise a welt across the fierce white sky. Jomama-Ploodle. Olin-Jay. Dix-Baedle. On their way back to the liner with stories of my demise. Could any product of their little minds be half so horrible as the truth? A race of serpents that kept humans in storage, buried alive, to use as "hands"!

The ache in the nape of my neck—yes, now I remembered. One of the snakes had bitten me there, sunk its fangs deep into my flesh. Tapped the spinal column, probably. Injected its sleep-inducing poisons. Hard to keep my eyes open. Might as well give in to it, slide down the hole, enjoy my sleep till the snakes came to get me.

Wait. Slithering sounds. Stay awake a minute longer—yes, there they were. Study them more closely now. Beady, intelligent eyes. Spoon-shaped heads the size of my fist. Quick, slick bodies quilted with scales. Sliding from side to side, tracing s-curves across the soil, cutting into the dirt around my body, carving me out of the ground. Feel them slithering against my skin. One of them climbing my back, my neck—ooow!—the bite. And they are inside me, bypassing the clumsy link of the larynx, plugging directly into my mind. A telepathic presence.

We have need of your hands.

49

What choice have I?

None. We have unburied your body. Now you must cross the plains of fleeza. You must walk to the mountains.

It's too far. I'll never reach them. I'm naked, I have no supplies. You've taken my clothes and my satchel and my boots.

We will drink the sacred waters of the fleeza and change it to whatever your body requires. We are adept at the transmutation of liquids.

Couldn't you please kill me instead?

The Urs do not kill.

Urs?

That is how we call ourselves.

But what about the Junglabarians?

You humans, you are the Junglabarians.

2

The Ur dangled from the nape of my neck; I could feel its wet body slapping against my spine as I walked. How long we had traveled I could not say. The distant peaks that rose purple and shimmering in the heat came no closer. The cloud cover hid the sun and diffused the light to a uniform brilliant whiteness. Even the sight of the sun would have given me no idea of time, for I did not know how fast the planet revolved. A day here might have been ten hours or it might have been a hundred.

More confusing still, I did not get tired! Perhaps the gravity was less, or the Ur was injecting stimulants through the curved hollow fangs that held it to my neck. Whatever the reason, I felt fabulously healthy. But it did seem a waste, this endless walking.

Why don't you have porta-walks or surface vehicles? I asked, forming the words in my mind.

Because we have no technology. Technology is the death of the spirit.

Is your civilization so primitive you don't even have the wheel?

It is typical of humans to equate a lack of technology with primitiveness. Technology expands and facilitates the capabilities of the body—the physiological. But the physiological is merely the tool of the spirit. The spirit is all-important. It is only through the spirit that we may find fulfillment. By glorifying the physiological with technology, the spirit is neglected and ultimately forgotten. The means to fulfillment become ends in themselves.

I think that's borselshit. It seems to me the real reason you don't have technology is that you don't have hands.

This is true, and it is a blessing. If we had hands we would certainly have developed into a technological civilization—the temptation would have been too great. But since we do not have hands, our evolution is confined to the spirit.

Well, if you're so spiritually evolved, why do you keep humans for slaves? We outlawed slavery thousands of years ago.

You have outlawed slavery? We think not. We probe the minds of the humans who come to hunt us. Each and every one of them is in bondage to a corporation.

You've misunderstood. Contracts aren't bondage. We enter into them willingly. The corporations are like parents. They take care of their employees and pay them a salary. That's not slavery.

If a man chooses to put himself into bondage, that does not make him less of a slave. If a master chooses to keep his slaves healthy enough to work, he is still a master. You are a slave of the Urs, that is true, but there is justice to it. Listen, that you may understand.

Two hundred years ago we traveled the universe at will. We did not use ships of metal, for we had a psychic energizer, a power stone, which enabled us to project our spirits through the farthest reaches of time/space. We were wonderfully free. We were never lonely, for we knew a million other civilizations and shared our knowledge with them.

Then the humans came in their metal ships—machines that had required centuries of labor to perfect. It seemed such a noble effort and so pitifully pointless. For every being contains within himself the potential for space travel.

So the humans came. We tried to show them their own spirits. We tried to teach them to travel the stars without machines. But they were blinded by their own technology. They could not relate to a kind of existence so different from

their own. Rather than try to understand us they made us int
monsters in their own minds. Junglabarians. They hunted u
for sport. They burned the fleeza. But their most obscen
their most blasphemous act was to take our power stone—th
catalyst of our freedom—and drop it in a crater atop the high
est peak on the planet. It was as if our freedom was unbear
able to them, as if they wanted to enslave us as they ha
enslaved themselves.

And so, for two hundred years we have been imprisone
on our planet, trapped here, cut off from the rest of the un
verse. And now, when humans come to hunt us, we giv
them the opportunity to undo the acts of their ancestors. W
let them try to retrieve our power stone. So far all hav
failed. Still we do not kill. We put them to sleep. When th
time comes that a human can retrieve our power stone, w
will wake them all and give them their liberty. It is a gentl
vengeance, you must agree.

Humans did that to you?

Yes.

Your story—it reminds me of something. I wish I coul
remember. Yes, yes, I know! A myth I learned in schoo
about two people who lived in a garden. They were at perfec
peace with the universe until a snake came, tempting ther
with evil—

Typically human. But enough for now. Lie down. Yo
must rest. Tomorrow you will have to walk a great distanc
You will have to reach the mountains. You will try to re
trieve our power stone.

3

The fierce brightness woke me. I wanted to raise my hand t
rub the crust of sleep from my eyes, but the Ur had left m
drugged, immobile. I was lying on the hard ground near
fleeza. Seven Urs formed a star at the base, their spoon
shaped heads arched to press fast against the stem. As
watched, one curved away from the plant and weaved towar

ne, tracing "S"s across the parched soil. It slid up my back
and bit my neck. I was no longer alone.

*Stand up. Begin to walk. We must reach the mountains be-
ore nightfall.*

Are you the same one who was with me yesterday? Your
voice is the same. But you seem smaller.

*The Ur is one. We are of a body. When I speak the Ur
speaks. When I listen the Ur hears.*

How is that possible?

*The fleeza has many leaves, but it is one plant. We are as
he leaves of the fleeza.*

Why are there always seven of you grouped around the
fleeza?

*Seven must congregate to drink the sacred waters. Seven
gives us strength. So it is intended in the design.*

The design? What is the design?

The design is as it is and as it must be.

Who made the design?

The Planner.

Who is the Planner?

The creator of life. The maker of the universe.

You mean God.

*Not God as you think of Him. We see in your mind an
image of God as a corporate head whose office is in the
clouds, who presides over a staff of executive angels, who tal-
lies our deeds and misdeeds in a computer and passes out the
rewards accordingly, like paychecks. We also see that you do
not really believe in the existence of such a being. You consider him a quaint folktale, as well you might.*

Then who is the Planner? I'd like to become as wise as
you, so I could spent all day lying in the sun, sucking on a
fleeza.

*We will ignore your sarcasm. It is a typical human reac-
tion, a sign of fear, a way of guarding the mind from new
ideas. Listen, that you may understand:*

*In the beginning there was one self-conscious entity. Since
it was nothing but itself, there existed nothing external to it,
nothing from which it could grow or learn. This condition
was unbearable. So it divided itself in half to create conflict.
Conflict is the cornerstone of growth. When the duality grew
tiresome it divided itself into more parts and more parts.
Each part was conscious unto itself. Some of the parts were
fleeza. Some of the parts were Urs. Some of the parts were humans.*

You are one of the parts.

Now the situation is reversed. We—the parts—try to gather together to find again the whole. We search for the Planner, as we call him, though in reality we ourselves are the Planner. For the Urs this search consists of seven uniting at the base of a fleeza to drink the holy waters. We call this uniting of seven a traste. *For humans the process may be different. We do not know. Humans themselves don't seem to know. If they ever did know they have certainly forgotten. This ignorance of purpose is the reason all humans live in frustration. This is the reason they envy and resent and eventually try to destroy anything that does understand its purpose in the universe. Even the isolated individuals within the human race who begin to perceive the purpose are ridiculed, persecuted, exterminated. What makes it all the sadder is that humans do not realize what they are doing. The rationalization for their own existences is so tenuous, they must blind themselves to everything that threatens it.*

4

Evening came and the mountains towered over us, rugged peaks of purple stippled with a yellowish moss. The sun slipped behind them and they became inky silhouettes against a violet sky. Their zigzag shadows crept across the plain, engulfing us. It grew cold. The Ur left me and went to suck at one solitary fleeza, the only plant we'd seen in hours.

When I rose in the morning I nearly fell over backward from its weight on my neck. It had drunk heavily during the night, storing enough to nourish us both through our climb and descent—for no fleeza grew in those rugged peaks. I had difficulty keeping my balance and took a while getting used to it before starting my climb.

I felt no fatigue. All that day I scaled the mountainside like a Kimba bear scampering up a brinko tree. Soon the height was dizzying. Perspective flattened the peaks below into piles of shattered glass. A false step would be fatal.

Now the side of the mountain grew smooth, except for an escarpment that wound up the rock face with such an easy slope, it might have been chiseled by man. Only care had to be taken: the ledge was narrow and carpeted with slippery moss. The weight of the Ur on my back didn't help any.

The ledge became narrower and I had to put one foot in front of the other to walk. On my left was a sheer drop of perhaps 2,000 feet. I tried not to look down for the sweep of the planet made my head spin, the endless expanse of ocher plain, the fleeza with spokes of Ur like tiny rimless wheels.

The ledge grew narrower still. I took small steps, testing the moss as I went along. It was slippery as oil under my bare feet. I dug in my toes for traction.

I'm turning back.

No. Go a little farther. Around the next bend you will see an outcropping of rock. You will be able to leap to it from the end of the ledge. From there on the climb to the peak is simple.

But the moss is so damned slippery!

It does not like to be walked on.

Well, I don't like to walk on it.

I managed to creep around the bend, balancing on the slim, slippery ledge. There was the outcropping as the Ur had promised, but I doubted I could reach it. Imagine standing at the top of a staircase, the outcropping being the foot of the staircase; but instead of stairs, empty air. I would have to creep another twelve feet along the edge to be directly over it, and the ledge was barely a sliver. Even if I could reach that point and leap, the outcropping was covered with that awful yellow moss. I'd probably slip right off.

Enough procrastinating. I put my weight on the outside of my right foot and slowly, cautiously, brought around my left foot. Good. One step closer. Now I rested my weight on the inside of my left foot and raised my right foot, bending my left knee slightly to let it clear—oh no, too far!

I slipped sideways off the moss with the sickening feeling of the bottom falling out. I twisted and grabbed at the ledge, desperately trying to get a grip in the moss, but my fingers slipped through it, as dreams slip away when we wake and no amount of effort will recapture them, and I fell.

5

I stopped in midair with a jolt and a painful wrench of my right shoulder. The Ur had coiled its tail around my right wrist and somehow sunk its fangs in the ledge above my head. I was dangling from a living thread 2,000 feet in the air.

The thoughts from the Ur were faint, as if it were calling to me from across a great distance.

The outcropping is almost below you. Swing your weight. When you have sufficient momentum I will let go of the ledge. You will swing far enough to fall onto the outcropping.

Too far—I can't.

You have no choice.

I pushed and guided myself with my free hand against the rock face. I swung up—the fierce white sky swept down on me. Then it slipped away and there was upside-down ocher plain. White sky—ocher plain—back and forth—sky and plain—back and forth—sky and—

Now.

Suddenly the tension was gone from my arm. I hurtled through space, trying to aim for the outcropping, the splash of yellow rushing up at me. My heels hit first and slid across the moss. I spun around so my body was flat against it and dug in my fingers and remained in that position, clinging insanely, panting for breath, for several minutes.

I sat up and felt myself gingerly. All in one piece. I'd made it—I was still alive! I'd cheated death again, and I laughed out loud. But I had to thank the Ur, it was really the Ur who had saved my life. My Ur. What had become of it?

Ah, there was its tail still wrapped around my wrist. The rest of its body hung limp over the edge of the outcropping. I hauled it in as one might haul in a rope. I unwrapped the coils of tail from my wrist and straightened its body and laid it out on the moss and waited. It did not move.

I thought about making a blanket of moss to keep it warm—but it was a coldblooded creature. I might massage its heart, but where was its heart? Did it have a heart? I put my head next to it, hoping I might hear some faint telepathic message. It was then I noticed that one side of its spoon-shaped head was crushed in and oozing a thick yellow sap.

6

An hour later I was standing at the top of the highest peak, looking down into the bowl of a crater. At the bottom I could see a shallow pool of lava, churning and bubbling lazily. And then I understood why no human had succeeded in retrieving the power stone—it lay submerged in the molten liquid.

I wanted to bring back the power stone, I wanted to help them. The Ur I had left below, growing stiff and dry on a deathbed of yellow moss, had nourished me and taught me and saved my life.

How simple it would have been if they had had even the most primitive tools, a pair of longhandled tongs, or a metal spoon. Even heat-resistant gloves. But the Urs had none of these, and so I stood there naked and alone and filled with despair at my own helplessness.

Then it came to me. Of course! I slapped my forehead at my own stupidity. The answer was obvious as the nose on my face, but it's always those obvious things, those things you live with from day to day, that you tend to forget.

I eased myself over the edge of the crater and slipped down the side. There was a bank around the lava where I could stand, although the rock was painfully hot. Above, the mouth of the crater cut a sharp circle of sky. I started to sweat. The smell of the lava made the inside of my nose burn.

I knelt on the rock bank, trying to ignore my burning knees, leaned forward over the pool and immersed my hand—my heat-resistant bionic hand. The lava came up to my wrist, almost to my flesh. I closed my fingers around a shape. I lifted it out of the pool.

It looked like a common piece of rock, but then the lava began to drip away and I saw that I was holding the most fabulous jewel. It was a seven-sided crystal the size of an egg, which pulsed with a light of its own, a cool blue iridescence.

The light bathed me, and in that instant my conditioning—all that I had ever been taught about perceiving myself and the universe and the interplay between the two—slipped away, as the lava had dripped from the power stone.

I saw the universe with the eyes of my spirit. I saw that everything the Ur had told me was a lie—for all words, all thoughts, are only the clumsiest approximations of the Truth. Now I was seeing the Truth itself. I knew. I understood. The world I lived in was a dream, a workable fabric of concepts. This peak, this crater, this pool of lava, all insubstantial, ephemeral. The Truth was a web of brilliant connecting fibers. Golden ropes of power. The fibers formed a nexus at the power stone clutched in my fist, and fanned off in every direction. One of the fibers connected to my solar plexus—I was a part of it.

All this happened in an instant, and the instant lasted an eternity. For time was simply another workaday concept that did not apply here. Then things were as they had been. The crater, the lava, the power stone. The heat. Ouch! I jumped to my feet. The heat was all too real—my knees were red and about to blister. This world may have been ephemeral, .but it could hurt.

7

I was climbing down a lower peak, the power stone pressed in my armpit to free my hands, when I noticed the Urs gathering below me. They came from every direction, amassing like pins at the pole of a magnet. Soon there was a dark, solid sea of them, and I could feel the excitement even from my perch hundreds of feet overhead. They were the prisoners; I came with the key to the universe.

When I reached the ground they had to move back to make space for me, so close to the base of the mountain had they crowded in anticipation. Their excitement seeped into my head, an overwhelming sensation, like standing under a waterfall.

I held out the stone in my fist. The roar in my skull grew louder, more frenetic. A very large Ur slithered in front of me and leaped up on its tail. Its gleaming fangs snapped at the stone, but I pulled back my hand. The roar subsided. The atmosphere grew quiet. Puzzled. Impatient.

Yet I was not afraid. I did not understand the power stone, but I could feel its force. And I knew intuitively that as long as I held it no act of the Urs could make me give it over. I formed words in my mind:

Unbury the other humans. Bring them here to me.

They are three days' distant. We cannot wait that long!

You have waited two hundred years. You will wait another three days.

8

The sea of Urs parted, leaving an ocher path, and twelve human figures came trudging toward me—though they were hardly human at all, more simian with their heavy beards and hair past their shoulders. They were naked as myself, and their faces were like oiled wood, but from the neck down they were nearly white, a curious effect of the manner in which they had been buried. Cowering and fearful they came, as if I were a king and they my subjects, trudging up a red carpet, coming to pledge their obedience.

All twelve of them knelt at my feet and rubbed their faces in the dirt to show humility. One man, older and more grizzled than the rest, lifted his head to speak. Long ago something had cut a gash across his cheek, taking his left eye in the process. No cosmetic surgeons had wasted time prettying him up. His voice cracked from disuse and trembled with fear.

"God bless you for freeing us! God bless you, boy. Whatever we can do, you tell us. We're your slaves for life."

Slaves. They had been freed and all they could think about was enslaving themselves again!

"*No!*" I shouted. "I've done nothing for you—you owe me *nothing!* I brought back the stone for the Urs. It's the Urs who deserve their freedom—we humans are too stupid to know what to do with it."

Saying this, I hurled the power stone into the air. A wave of Urs rose to catch it. Then the snakes moved away from us, moved as a whole like some giant, jellyish amoeba, the power stone pulsing from within like a cool blue heart. The roar of their excitement threatened to split my skull.

The twelve men were still kneeling at my feet.

"Get up!" I snapped. "Stop acting like borsels. Where's your dignity?"

Timidly they rose. They were watching me as if I were a creature stranger than the Urs.

The grizzly one said, "Beg your pardon, boy, but you saved us. You did a miracle. You picked the power stone out of the lava."

"It's no miracle, you idiot. I have a bionic hand. It's heat-resistant plastic."

He turned his one good eye on my hand, but he wasn't convinced.

"It's not just your hand," said another, younger man. "It's your eyes. There's something about your eyes."

He hesitated. They were all staring at me. I felt uncomfortable. Had my *vision* left its mark? Or was it simply a projection on his part, making me into something special because I had saved him?

"You're different from us," he said.

9

This young man's name was Alan-Tal, and he was gentle and soft-spoken, almost girlish with long blond locks which he tugged at incessantly.

He and his partner, Del-Rae, a quiet, withdrawn man several years his senior, worked for the AUAR—the Aid for Underveloped Alien Races. I knew a little about the organization. It was funded by the United Board of Corporations, and critics of UltraCap had accused it of being a propaganda tool. I didn't know if this was so, but I could tell that Alan-Tal was sincere and kind and helpful to a fault, and I imagined that he had joined the AUAR with entirely humanitarian motives.

Now another man came forward. Black hair and a beard streaked with silver framed his aristocratic face. He had a dark, brooding stare and a voice one obeyed without question. His name was Ben-Gotz and he and his two companions had been shipwrecked here and taken by the Urs—that was all he would say. But his guarded manner led me to believe there was much more.

The other seven—including the grizzly old fellow whose grizzly name was Sak-Zpfitle—were professional hunters, and a worse bunch of rogues I'd never hope to meet. Crude, foul-mouthed, belligerent. They started bragging to me about the high fees they earned, and in a moment they were bickering about who got paid the most—and in another moment they would have been at each other's throats, if I hadn't interceded.

Then they took turns boasting about how cleverly they tricked their employers, stashing "'barian scalps" in their satchels at the start of a safari (one used strips of gilligator hide dyed black, another apploupe rind soaked in blood) and bringing them back later as proof of the kill.

They were scoundrels indeed. Then I recalled that I too had been a hunter, briefly, and delighted with the idea of cheating my employers, those bastards. So perhaps the nature of the game was more to blame than the players.

Now it came my turn. I talked vaguely of my past and more specifically of my present, describing my adventures since arriving on the planet in great detail. I mentioned what the Ur had told me about space flight without ships, and when I had finished, several of the men had me go back to that and repeat the conversation as best I could remember it. Certainly it was an outrageous idea, an idea that strained credibility to the breaking point. But desperate men will grasp at the slimmest hope. And we were desperate, marooned in a remote sector of the galaxy, far from the commercial trade routes, with no means of summoning help and perhaps years to wait before the next hunting party set down on Jungla-besh's parched soil.

I told them that flying without ships was a mystery that might take lifetimes to unravel. Foolish to waste time thinking about it.

"You may be closer to the solution than you think," Ben-Gotz interrupted. "During the latter part of the twenty-second century an esoteric sect called the Wanderers claimed to have perfected a technique for astral projection. They were considered a threat to capitalism and were exterminated during the Great Corporate Revolution of 2412."

"Ain't that interesting," Sak-Zpfitle grumbled. "Tickled to think we're sitting here on a slimy *repteelian* planet, having a chugga-fugging history lesson!"

"If you'll shut up for a minute," Ben-Gotz said in measured tones, "I'll explain the importance of it."

Sak-Zpfitle fell silent and stared at his hands like a scolded schoolboy.

"Those Wanderers spoke of crossing the universe on a ladder of golden ropes. It was metaphor, I suppose, but what interests me is the way it jibes with your description of—"

"Of what I saw when I rescued the power stone. Yes, the strands of power. The golden ropes. And you think that might be how it's done—by following the strands of power?"

"Honestly," Ben-Gotz said, "I don't know. It's possible."

"Do you think you could do it?" Alan-Tal asked eagerly. He brushed the long locks from his face. "You could get help. You could have somebody send a rescue ship."

"I'm not sure I could see the golden ropes again, and even if I could, the traveling must require special skills. One thing's for sure—I'd have to have the power stone. And I don't suppose the Urs are going to feel like giving it up, not after waiting so long."

"Don't expect nothing from them slimy snakes," Sak-Zpfitle grumbled. "They're chugga-fugging *repteelians*!"

Alan-Tal laid a restraining hand on the hunter's arm.

"That's a bad attitude. The Urs may be reptiles, but they've been pretty decent to us, considering the circumstances."

Sak-Zpfitle shook off the hand as if it were a snake's scaly touch.

"You know what I think?" He swung his head around to train his single eye on each of us in turn. "I think it's a crock of overcooked borselshit. Spaceflight without ships. Bah! Truth is, we're stuck on this chugga-fugging planet with those chugga-fugging *repteelians* for the rest of our chugga-fugging lives!"

Ben-Gotz glared. "If you have any more thoughts on the matter, I suggest you keep them to yourself."

"Or else?" the hunter demanded.

Ben-Gotz said nothing, just kept staring at him.

Sak-Zpfitle turned to the other six hunters for support, but they were picking at their nails and scratching their beards and otherwise avoiding his eye. After a minute, he got up and stalked away, muttering, "*Repteel* lóvers—"

That evening when the Urs came to feed us—the telepathic connection was stronger then—I told them I wished to use the power stone to attempt to travel through space and find a rescue ship.

After a long silence they replied:

We understand your longing for your own culture. Come morning you may have the power stone for half a day.

10

One large Ur stopped at my feet and balanced on its tail. I took the stone from its jaw and the blue light of it chilled my fingertips. The twelve men watched at a distance as though afraid they might be yanked into space with me if I succeeded and they were standing too close.

I tried to feel precisely what I had felt on the mountain top, the same sense of exhilaration and peace, of triumph at retrieving the stone and humility in the face of the Urs' momentous wisdom. Then I held up the stone and gazed into its cool depths.

Gradually the rhythm of its pulsating light became the rhythm of my existence—and suddenly the world gave way and again I beheld the golden ropes of power, the bedrock truth beneath the slit of my perceptions, one strand penetrating my solar plexus, an infinitude of others converging into the facets of the power stone.

I don't know how I did it; I could no sooner explain how I made my heart beat or forced the blood to course through my veins. I concentrated my entire being on the strand that penetrated my solar plexus, and the next instant I felt a sickening wrench in my stomach and then I was someplace else.

A long, dark room, the strands of power glowing through it, giving the scene an eerie quality. I was perceiving both worlds simultaneously, the world of everyday reality, and the world of a greater, more basic reality. My intellectual mind existed in the first world, my intuitive mind—my *will*—in the second. Yet I could deal with both worlds at once without any confusion, *for they were actually two aspects of the same thing.*

I looked across the room, the rows of hammocks crowded one on top of the next, the children moaning, turning restlessly in their sleep—I was in the Digger barracks on Slabour!

I heard a weeping. I perceived a golden form, a mushroom shape, twisted by sadness. And I saw a boy sitting on his hammock, holding his face in his hands. He looked up, squinting in the darkness.

"Stefin? Is that you?"

"Yes, Mo."

"But—how? The security guards—they killed you when you tried to escape. That's what Boss Callow said."

"He lied, Mo. I escaped. I'm living on another planet, but somehow my spirit came here to see you."

"Your spirit?"

"There isn't time to explain. Believe me, though, I'm alive."

Mo sniffed and wiped his eyes. He squinted at me again

and then he smiled. The golden mushroom of his being glowed brighter.

"You *are* alive! Oh Stefin, I'm so glad! I thought I was all alone now—you dead, then today Simon—my two best friends—"

"What about Simon?"

"He talked back to Boss Callow's eye. I guess Callow just meant to sting him, but something must have gone wrong with the machinery—the eye kept on firing and Simon was lying there twitching, like somebody was sticking pins in him."

His voice dissolved in sobs. "Shipped home—he's shipped back home. . . ."

"Easy, Mo," I whispered. "He's gone to hunt with Orion, and drink from the Dipper, and charm the skirts off the Pleiades."

"The Pleiades." Mo managed a smile. "Seven sisters—you think Simon can handle them?"

I grinned. "Sure." Then I wasn't grinning any more. "Mo, I can't take you with me now, but I'll be back for you, I swear it. I'll come back and take you away from here and all the other Diggers too. And I'll make Boss Callow suffer for every Digger he's ever stung. Tell me, Mo, what happened to Suki?"

"Suki?" He stared at me dumbly.

"My Scrugal. The pretty one with the sad eyes."

"Oh her. The Scrulux Police came. They had a beautiful ship, all black and shiny. And they took her away—I don't know where. Stefin? Simon's shipped home. I'm scared."

"Don't be scared, Mo. I have to go now."

"No! Please stay with me—"

"I can't—I only have a little time. But I'll be back, I promise."

"Don't go, Stefin, don't leave me alone—"

Then again I felt the wrench in my stomach. And I was in a high tower, in a tiny cell with one window. A woman stood at the window looking out at a landscape of endless ocean. She wore a loose robe of coarse cloth. I saw her also as a slender spindle of gold, but the gold was tarnished by loneliness and despair.

"Suki," I whispered.

She spun around and stared at me with terror. The blood drained from her face. She began to laugh, and her laughter had a brittle edge.

"It's really me," I pleaded. "You're not dreaming and you're not crazy."

"Oh no." She shook her head savagely. "The solitude's gotten to me—I'm mad as a Murn and you're a little piece of my madness."

I tried to shake sense into her. But my hands passed through her flesh, and that scared her even more. So I explained everything, meeting the Urs, saving the power stone, being marooned and projecting my spirit, while she cowered from me, trembling with fear.

In time a dull-eyed quiet overcame her. Either she believed me, or she had simply decided to give in to the "delusion." I asked where we were, that I might soon rescue her—assuming I could first rescue myself.

"A prison planet," she said. "A water world."

"Do you know the coordinates? Or what sector it's in?"

She shook her head. "No, Stefin, no false hopes. That's too cruel." I saw a glimmer in her sad sad eyes, the dimmest reflection of how she had looked when we were lovers. "Forgive me. I'm older than you know. Not too many days left. Soon the Change will be upon me and I'll be no use to anyone."

"But I love you, Suki."

She made a painful smile. She reached out—but before her hand could touch my cheek I felt another violent jerk and I was standing on the parched soil of Junglabesh, gazing at the pulsing blue light of the power stone. My head reeled.

When the nausea subsided I looked around and the twelve men were sitting precisely as I'd left them. Only seconds had elapsed! I handed the stone to an Ur which was waiting by my feet and watched absently as it slithered away.

"Did it work?" Alan-Tal asked eagerly. "Did you contact a rescue ship?"

I hesitated, trying to focus my thoughts. "No. Nothing happened. I shrugged. "Looks like we're stuck here."

I *had* wanted to contact a rescue ship—I didn't want to stay on that awful planet any more than the rest of them. But traveling the golden ropes of power was not governed by what the mind desired. Rather, it was my spirit that guided the course. And my spirit brought me to Mo and Suki—they were the ones I longed to see. But I could not tell the twelve men that. How would I explain? They would feel betrayed, and doubly frustrated to know that while I could travel the universe, I could not consciously choose my destination.

After giving the matter some thought, I decided that this was not unique to the world of golden ropes; perhaps it also held true for the everyday world; that mind stands at the prow of the ship giving orders left and right, but the spirit is the secret steerer.

11

A smell woke me, a sickeningly sweet smell with an after-taste that made my toes curl. It was a smell of rotting fruit, of putrid flesh. The air, I saw, was thick with a saffron-colored smoke.

I was on top of a ridge where we had been sleeping for the past few weeks. The hunters insisted on sleeping here because the Urs kept to the flatlands. The rest of us were comfortable enough with the snakes, yet some primitive instinct huddled us together against the alien night. All along the ridge the men were cramped in awkward sleep, like corpses in the saffron smoky aftermath of a battle. I looked again and saw there were only eleven. Alan-Tal was gone.

Now I looked out over the flatlands. The smoke was thicker there; it rolled across the plain like folds of ghostly cloth. The fleeza was wilting. Spade-shaped leaves hung limp on withered stalks. Other plants trailed mournfully across the earth. Through the curling smoke Alan-Tal emerged, running toward me.

I clambered down the side of the ridge to meet him. He stopped before me, breathless, distraught.

"Stefin, the Urs—you've got to do something!"

He led me to a fleeza, a brown stringy plant that had dropped most of its leaves. Lying at the base were seven shriveled sticks. I had to look closely to see that they had once been Urs. Now their glassy skins were lusterless and dry. I turned one over with my toe and it was stiff.

"All of them," Alan-Tal said, "they're all like that. The whole planet's dead, Stefin, what's happened?"

"I don't know," I said. "This stuff in the air—do you smell it?"

He nodded and grimaced. "Some kind of poison gas. But how? Why?" His eyes were wet.

I shrugged. I held out my hands helplessly. I felt sadness like a great weight on my shoulders.

Presently the others joined us. We split into groups and went off in four directions searching for life. When we regathered several hours later, Sak-Zpfitle was carrying a limp Ur in his hands. The skin was dull and grainy, the eyes sunken into the skull. But the body still writhed in its deaththroes, and that was more life than any of the rest of us had found.

He handed it to me, muttering, "Poor old repteel, poor critter." Now that the Urs were dead and dying he seemed quite amiable toward them.

I held the spoon-shaped head to my temple and strained to form a telepathic link. After a moment I heard the voice of the Urs, a distant whisper.

Our bodies die, but the spirit lives. The spirit endures. You who saved the power stone, do not grieve, for death is in the design.

Silence. Then:

Your knowledge of the golden ropes is dangerous. It is a threat to the economic chains that bind the human spirit. Because of it other humans will try to destroy you.

A longer silence. Then the voice came once more, so faint I could barely understand it.

Have caution. Beware the secrets of synchronicity.

And then a silence that had no end.

12

That afternoon the earth trembled. Thunder shook some few remaining leaves off the fleeza, and a great silver pod fell gently from the sky. It settled several miles mountainward of where we watched, shielding our eyes from the glare, and we hiked toward the site.

It wasn't a shuttle: it was ten times the size of a shuttle. Four hatches were opened and men were driving tractorlike machines with enormous balloon tires down ramps. More machines were already at work, digging up scoops of earth, while others flattened the ground and still others stood by heaving and groaning and waiting to do who knew what next.

One man appeared to be supervising the operation. He wore bright-orange coveralls and a silver helmet, and chewed a cigar while he spoke orders into a lavaliere microphone. When he spotted us his jaw dropped open and the cigar fell out. He picked it up. He put it back between his teeth and said something into the microphone.

All action ceased. The machines fell silent and the men who were operating them climbed down from their bucket seats. They too wore the bright-orange coveralls and silver helmets, and when we were closer I could read the writing on their breast-pockets: *Trans-Galactic Realty And Construction.*

"Let me handle this," Ben-Gotz said in a low voice. He sized up the situation in an instant. Stepping to the front, he took control.

Remember, we were naked. I'd grown accustomed to it soon after being unburied and hadn't given it a thought since. But now, watching him approach the man with the cigar, our nakedness became of great consequence—a terrible psychological disadvantage. For the clothed man is an emblem of civilization and the naked man is a beast.

The fellow with the cigar smiled uncomfortably. He was big, burly and round-shouldered. Ruddy skin and thick features.

Ben-Gotz was half a head shorter, yet he confronted him with wonderful poise and self-assurance.

"What is the meaning of this?" he demanded.

With a wave of his arm he encompassed the landscape of wilting fleeza and rotting Urs, and the yellow gas that hung in the air like a bad conscience.

The man pushed back his helmet and scratched his brow. His smile grew more uncomfortable still.

"Weren't supposed to be any humans here."

"Well, there are humans here. And there was also a brilliant civilization of reptiles—until this morning."

The man stopped smiling. He took the cigar out of his mouth and shook the butt at Ben-Gotz.

"Listen, mister, we got orders last week to fly up here and

gas the place with Double M-437, then clean up and dig some foundations. Trans-Galactic Realty's got it all planned to put up condominiums here. There's something in the atmosphere makes people feel healthy. So they're gonna build a retirement community so old folks can benefit. We got plans to irrigate. Grass and flowers and trees. A lake with a marina. Eighteen-hole auto-golf course. Paddle-tennis courts and a shuffle-bluff field. Imagine how it'd be with those snakes jumping out of the bushes and scaring the skins off everybody." Perspiration beaded all over his ruddy face. "My orders come from up there. They pay me and I do what they tell me. It ain't my fault if—"

"Do you know," Ben-Gotz said in measured tones, "the penalty for genocide? The United Board of Corporations takes a dim view of it."

The sweat ran in rivulets.

"I swear to God, mister, it ain't my fault! You come in the ship and we'll call up my supervisor. You talk to him. I just go where they tell me."

Ben-Gotz left the man squirming over his fate, and took us aside. He spoke softly.

"By threatening to turn them in to the UBC I think I can get each of us a free trip home, and maybe a cash settlement too. But we all have to decide which way to go—whether to negotiate for a settlement or report them. The decision *has* to be unanimous. If one of us goes to the UBC afterward, then the rest of us will be in jeopardy for conspiring to cover up genocide. Now, I want you to remember, nothing we can do will bring the Urs back to life. What's done is done and vengeance and remorse have never profited anybody. I say we negotiate."

"Negotiate," agreed the two men who'd been marooned with him.

"Negotiate," said the hunters.

Alan-Tal looked at his partner, Del-Rae. Reluctantly, they agreed.

"Negotiate."

Everybody was watching me. I sighed. I didn't like it, but I felt I had to subordinate my wishes to those of the majority—it seemed like the only right thing to do.

"Negotiate."

At nightfall a weary Ben-Gotz emerged from the ship to tell us of the settlement. Each of us would be transported to

New Panama, the closest major warp-nexus, and from there to our home planets, free of charge, And each of us would receive 100,000 CUs as—what should I call it? A bribe? That's what it was.

Well, the hunters were ecstatic. They whooped and hollered and hugged each other. For the rest of us the death of the Urs was too recent, too awful. It was lodged in my chest like a shard of metal.

We were dressed in orange coveralls and fed a supper of real solid chewable swallowable food. That night we slept in hammocks, in the technological security of the ship.

Next morning I had time for a stroll before lift-off, and I went out alone and walked for miles across the ocher plains. Presently I came to a place where the ground was littered with the shriveled, sticklike bodies of the Urs. A pulsating, cool blue light caught my attention. I tiptoed between the bodies, trying not to step on them, picked up the power stone and sealed it in the pocket of my coveralls.

I did not look at it again until two days later, after the planet of the Urs had shrunk to a pinprick of light, lost among the silver dust spread of stars. Then I went to the toilet, the only place where I was assured of privacy, and opened the pocket. What I took out felt light and porous, like a lump of burned charcoal. The radiance was gone, the jewel had turned opaque, gray as ash. It crumbled in my hand and the fine powder trickled through my fingers.

Part IV

The Church of Bode-Satva

The man who covets power is hungry.
No amount of food will sate him.
His high pedestal rests upon a mountain
Of those with less appetite.
Do not lie down before him
Or you will find his footprint
On your back.
>   —The Holy Tapes of Bode-Satva
>   (Tape #112,518)

1

Wounds heal, memories fade. With every passing day the Urs grew more dreamlike while the wad of credit units bulging my pocket became more real and spendable. I actually began to anticipate the return to human civilization.

My friendship with Alan-Tal made the trip almost pleasant. We were similar enough in age and attitude to carry on a conversation, different enough to keep it interesting. He was a *Boozhie*, the son of a wealthy merchant, an importer of Pik. He'd been coddled, catered to, forced to do nothing all his childhood. That, I decided, was the cause of the great guilt he felt toward all the less fortunate. He was a hopeless do-gooder. Now he was having a crisis of conscience, sitting with me in the ship's lounge, trying to decide whether to leave the AUAR.

The lounge was a private place, thanks to the observation bubble, a thick plastic blister that stretched the stars at its edge. The others didn't like the sight of the velvet blackness and kept away. There were stories about space-watching, about the rapture of the void that drove seasoned spacers to leave their ships unsuited. Stories or no, I liked it. It gave me a good feeling, a feeling that life went on and on and that this body I lived in, this *Stefin-Dae*, was only the beginning and not the all. When you feel like that you're not scared of dying, only respectful of it. And when you're not scared of dying, that's the only time you can really be alive.

Ben-Gotz frequented the lounge too. He had programmed the computer terminal in that room for an ancient speckers variation. Now you may think that speckers is a simple, pleasurable pastime fit for children and doddering old men. But this variation mimicked corporate warfare in all its complexity. One piece, for example, the "King," represented the Prez. Other pieces were Vice-Prezes and Comptrollers and Attorneys. Then there were a number of pieces called "Pawns" that represented the workers. Ben-Gotz gave me a lesson or two. I tried my hand and the computer beat me in seven moves!

But when Ben-Gotz played, the games went on for hours. He was playing now, bent over the console, and from his expression you might have thought the fate of the galaxy hung on every move. Only a grunt or snort or mutter reminded us he was in the room—and made me wonder that a man so calm in the crisis of life could get so worked up playing games with a machine.

"I can't go back to the AUAR," Alan said for the third or fourth time that afternoon. "I can't."

"Then don't," I said.

"They tricked me, you know. They told me I'd be helping aliens reap the benefits of human technology—when really I was laying foundations for wage slavery. I was so naive. But the incident with the Urs opened my eyes. The thought of those beautiful, holy snakes being defiled by our materialist—"

"So don't go back," I said, for the fourth or fifth time that afternoon.

"Well, maybe I won't."

"Why all this *maybeing*?"

"Because . . . well, because . . ." Alan fidgeted and tugged at a strand of hair. Then it poured out: "Because I don't know what else to do! I don't have a profession. I don't have any goals—except making the galaxy a better place to live."

That sounded a little vague.

From the back of the lounge came a triumphant "Hah!" and "Check!"

"I'm not finished yet," the computer replied in its grinding voice. "You're trapped by your own Queen's Knight."

"Maybe," Ben-Gotz muttered. "And maybe not."

"Listen," I said. "I don't know what to do either. But I'm not agonizing over it."

"You don't need to, Stefin. You're different. You take life as it comes. I've got to have a course mapped out. Otherwise I feel . . . *insecure*."

"Checkmate."

"You snuck up on me, Ben-Gotz. I'm wise to you now." The computer sounded petulant. "Another game. Play me another."

"Not now, old friend," Ben said, patting the terminal. "Run the ship for a while. Earn your keep."

"Soon then?"

"Tomorrow," Ben agreed.

He walked over to the cola dispenser and, without dropping in a single Cu, removed three chilled bottles.

"How do you do that?" Alan-Tal asked, craning around in his chair.

"The computer controls the vending machine. I get five colas every time I win a game."

"What happens," I asked, "when the machine wins?"

"It hasn't yet—and it won't. Computers are consistent," Ben continued. "They're perfectly logical and totally devoid of imagination. It's people you have to watch out for."

He handed me a nutra-cola and gave one to Alan. Then he sat down across from us, uninvited. He stared at us and I felt as if he were peeling back my skull like fruit rind and looking straight into my brain.

He said, "You've been wondering about me, haven't you? Who I am. How I came to be marooned on Junglabesh."

Of course we had.

"Five years ago," he continued, "I was elected President of Nova Spacecraft."

He gave that a moment to sink in. Yes, now that I thought about it, even the orange coveralls could not hide his executive bearing. He was clearly a ruler of men—or so it seemed in retrospect.

"The election was close," he went on. "I defeated my opponent, Urtz-Al, by the vote of one powerful shareholder. My first act after coronation was to institute work-incentive bonuses. Production had been declining, and I assumed that would rectify it.

"Urtz-Al saw a second chance. He interpreted my plan as a form of profit-sharing and therefore anti-cap in principle. He denounced me at a board meeting. He called for my resignation—that would have throned him in my place. Then came the proclamation for the first quarter: production up eight percent. Profit vincit omnia. I was a hero. Urtz-Al came to my throne room in person to apologize for the . . . *ideological error*. That's what he called it.

"Several months passed and I had to visit our research center on Cebes 5 to watch tests of a new engine. I invited Urtz-Al to join me. A political gesture, you understand, to heal old wounds. Quite traditional and proper. We took my private yacht.

"After breakfast the third day in space I noticed a heaviness in my limbs. Another hour passed before I guessed the truth—Urtz-Al had bribed the crew to slip a paralytic in my stimu-caff. By then it was too late. I couldn't move. I had to listen helplessly while Urtz-Al taunted me with his plans.

"He had forged records showing I was an embezzler. He would tell the board that he had confronted me with this 'evidence' and rather than return dishonored, I had taken my own life. Then he laughed at me, he laughed in my face—and for that I'll see him die the slowest, most agonizing death I can arrange.

"Later that day he abandoned us, myself and my two Protectionists—a lot of use they were—on a world called Junglabesh, populated by creatures with no appreciation of corporate justice."

"That's awful!" Alan said. "But now you can take the throne again, can't you?"

"Only with evidence clearing my name."

"What kind of evidence?" I asked.

"I'd had my yacht bugged. A recording system went on every time anyone entered a room. Paranoia," he added cynically, "is only one of the prices of power. *If* the recorder wasn't discovered, and *if* my yacht wasn't destroyed—well then, evidence *may* exist."

Two *if*s and a *may*. It didn't sound good to me.

"I couldn't help overhearing," Ben-Gotz continued, "how neither of you had any plans. Urtz-Al mustn't find out I'm alive. I'll have to go into hiding. Someone must recover the tape for me." He hesitated. "Two would be better."

I remembered a chess strategy Ben-Gotz had shown me called the "Poisoned Pawn." The Pawn, a little nobody, gets sacrificed for the sake of the King. "Thanks for the cola," I said, and got up to leave.

"Wait a minute," Alan said. "This man needs our help. He doesn't have anybody else to turn to."

I kept walking.

"If you can recover the tape," Ben-Gotz said, "I'll give you the yacht and anything else I can—within reason."

I had a vision of myself at the helm, swooping down on a prison planet and rescuing Suki, then on route to Slabour armed with a battery of 30-millimeter blasters that would turn Boss Callow's tower to a fine dust and him along with it.

I sat back down.

2

Next morning we docked at New Panama, a planet located at the nexus of several major warp-routes and the busiest port in this sector. Space crafts swarmed the skies like insects around a sweet. Thousands of Class W ships, too huge to land, were moored to orbiting dry docks, and lower down where the sky turned smoky blue the shuttles were so numerous I feared midair collisions. But our landing pattern steered us safely between them and we touched ground, wonderfully firm underfoot. Porta-walks to the terminal building. Customs and DeContam. Special "Castaway Clearance" courtesy Trans-Galactic Realty. No, no luggage.

I went to the shopping arcade in the terminal and bought a depili-shave and a hair trim, and in the next store, three embroidered caftans. I had a shock, trying one on in front of the mirror. Could that be me, that fashionable fellow? He looked so old. And his eyes had the strangest light to them.

Strolling around the terminal that afternoon, I came across several of the hunters. They were boarding a liner bound for Vargas, an amusement planet—if murder, rape and torture constitute your idea of amusement. It sure didn't tigger my circuits. They all thanked me for saving them and hoped we would meet again someday, a sentiment I could not honestly say I shared. Sak-Zpfitle almost missed the flight. Last I saw of him he was stumbling down the gangplank with a five-gallon tank of lixor under each arm and an equal amount—judging from the way he collided with the stewardess—in his belly.

Later I met Alan and Del-Rae in the plush, dark lixor lobby. Del shared none of Alan's disillusionment with the AUAR. As far as he could see, progress meant technology and production—hence the Urs were underdeveloped aliens. His only regret was that the snakes had been annihilated before he had had an opportunity to "civilize" them.

He had transmitted news of their failure—and Alan's resignation—to AUAR Center. They scolded him, assigned him a partner with a "less negative attitude" and arranged passage to a frontier planet where dwelled virgin aliens whose limber tentacles might be taught to hold tools. Del would embark within the hour.

Despite their differences it was an amiable parting, Del-Rae was the sort of man who needed to be part of an organization. Direction, discipline, a galactic view—resources some of us could find within ourselves, he had to receive from without. Alan understood and did not hold it against him, any more than he would have blamed a crippled man for not being able to skip.

3

That evening Alan and I stepped into a transparent cylinder; the door rotated shut and we hurtled up a transparent tube that climbed the outside of the terminal building. The acres and acres of landing fields, crisscrossed with necklaces of light, shrank below us. Shuttles passed parallel to us, shooting stars with white-hot tails.

We got out at the 239th floor, the top of the terminal. Synthi-grass sloped gently between three levels of tiers where tables were set, each glowing warm with its own candle. A clear dome overhead let in the stars and kept out much of the rocket noises. A waterfall wall helped too, spilling into a lagoon where doll-fish played.

The maitre d', an elegant robot, led us to a table on the highest tier. Ben-Gotz was already there, waiting. We ordered and he got down to business directly:

"You've decided?"

"We'll do it."

"First thing tomorrow both of you must become shareholders."

"Can we?"

It seemed inconceivable. Me, Stefin-Dae, a shareholder!

"Of course. Anyone can. All you have to do is buy stock.

There's a Bank-of-the Cosmos on the forty-ninth floor of the terminal building. You will contact the broker there and buy one share of Nova Spacecraft apiece. Technically that will give you access to Management Hill when you arrive at Nova Center. The only ship bound for there this month is a freighter. I took the liberty of booking you passage. The accommodations aren't deluxe, but it should suffice."

Stefin-Dae the Digger wouldn't have minded, but Stefin-Dae the *shareholder*—well, he'd try to tolerate the inconvenience.

"What happens," Alan asked, "when we get there?"

Three Muzackers who had set up instruments by the lagoon began to tease sounds from their fragile glass reeds. A spotlight hit the top of the waterfall where a naked woman balanced on one toe and followed her as she slid down and down and into the lagoon with hardly a splash.

Ben-Gotz didn't waste a glance on her.

"Executives," he continued, "change loyalties as easily as they change caftans. Trust no one. Go to the palace guard and tell him you want an appointment with Arel-Spline, the Comptroller. Say it is urgent and you must see him immediately. Arel-Spline was my personal accountant before he took his present post. He alone can be trusted."

The lagoon water was luminous. It clung to the woman when she climbed out, stippling her shape with a million scintillae. She did a sensual dance, dripping light, spraying showers of fire from her fingertips. Slowly she climbed to the first tier, then the second, never losing time with the music. This did not help my concentration.

"You may not speak freely, even when you are alone with Arel-Spline. His office is bugged—I know this for certain because I ordered the bugging myself."

"Wait a second," I said, forcing my attention away from the dancer. "If he's the only one you trust, why did you bug his office?"

"I bugged everyone's office. Not to bug his would have made him suspect."

"Oh," I said. "I see." Though I didn't really.

"Tell him to meet you in the evening at a lixor lobby called the White Dwarf. It's on a back street in the Valley of the Workers—you won't have trouble finding it. It's a noisy, rowdy place where you won't be overheard."

The woman danced past our table, weaving and turning, watching our reactions over her shoulder. Every man, woman

and robot under that dome was locked in the spell of he
dance. Except Ben-Gotz. She passed the table again, trying t
get his attention. Anger flashed in her amber eyes. Her dusk
skin was velvet. The third time she came to a stop behin
Ben's chair and started tossing drops of glowing water on hi
head. The other diners began to snicker. Ben kept right o
talking. The water began to trickle down his forehead, an
Ben wiped it away with a finger and kept on talking. Peopl
were laughing now. The woman took advantage of it an
mimed the part of the neglected wife whose husband is to
busy to scru. Her face was marvelously comic and expressive
I started laughing despite myself.

Then Ben whipped around and I thought he would strik
her, I really did, but instead he glowered; and the hate in hi
eyes was such that it tore away the veil of her art, the magi
of her dance, and left her plainish and awkward like th
fairytale princess whose enchantment has worn off.

For the longest moment nobody moved or made a sound
Then the other diners picked up their conversations. Th
woman slunk away. Ben-Gotz turned back to us and said:

"When you meet at the White Dwarf, tell him I'm sti
alive. Tell him you have to recover the tapes from my yach
to prove my innocence. He'll determine the next move. D
you have that?"

I nodded, hoping Alan had been more attentive. I'd hardl
heard a word.

4

Thirty-four days later we arrived on Nova Center and too
an airbus from the landing field to Management Hill. Ala
sat beside me murmuring, "What am I doing here... I mus
be out of my mind . . . wonder if they'd take me back a
AUAR ..." and so forth. Meanwhile I pressed my nose t
the cool curved green window and watched the land unrol
below me. It was easy to see why Nova Space craft ha

chosen this planet for a base—the natural resources were re-markable.

We passed over mines where green earth had been stripped away, leaving black ribbons like the filling between layers of a cake. Mechanical worms wriggled down holes which must have reached all the way to the planet's core. And here is an interesting fact the airbus driver told us:

Ten years before, the mass of the planet had given it gravity of 2.1G. In other words, a man weighing 170 pounds StandardGrav, weighed 357 pounds on Nova Center. Workers had to wear lighteners, and even then they tired quickly. But so much of the planet's minerals had been mined since then—so much of her insides had been hollowed out—that now the gravity was 1.4G. He who had weighted 357 pounds ten years ago weighed 238 pounds today. Needless to say, this played havoc with certain dieting wives on Management Hill. Over the years their scales read the same, but their girth grew and grew. Which had led to arguments, fights, even a few divorces—or so claimed our airbus driver. Although I thought I detected a twinkle in his eye.

We passed over mills and refineries, bellowing smoke. Presently the smoke was so thick it might have been night. All I could distinguish was a glowing thread. Ford River according to the driver, iridescent with radioactive wastes. When the sky cleared again the river looked black. It wound its way through parched canyons and flowed finally into Carnegie Ocean, leaving a delta of slick black sludge in its wake.

What poor little planet had ever suffered such abuse at the hands of man? How sad that stone has no voice to complain, no hands to brush the vermin off her skin. Yet I think justice is a natural force like gravity or magnetism, and those who defile the galaxy today will be brought to task tomorrow.

We passed factories, endless rows of identical buildings and fields where ships of every description lay end to end, smooth and sensual as sleeping women.

And finally we flew over a great valley of ramshackle shacks and crazy cobblestone streets, all decrepit and oddly angled, as if man had never invented the spirit level or plumb line, and landed atop a mountain in the shadow of a vast fortress as upright and solid as old Adam Smith himself. Welcome to Management Hill.

5

If ever anything had been designed to intimidate, it was the entrance to the Executive Palace. The doors were thirty feet high and carved from some sapphire stone. The golden knobs were the size of my head. The hinges, if detached and laid flat, would have made spacious sleep-slabs.

A stone kiosk stood off to one side. At least it looked like stone, but when we came closer, I could see that it was formed from sheets of plastic, cunningly embossed to simulate stone. Perhaps the whole palace was similarly constructed, like certain people I had met whose imposing facades had little to back them. The kiosk had a thick window behind which sat the Palace Guard. He switched on an intercom and spoke to us through a tinny speaker.

"What can I do for you?"

"We're—" I began.

"Don't tell me," he said. "New recruits for the Executive Training Corps—am I right?" He nodded sagely. "Been here thirty years, I can spot 'em in a second."

"Actually—" I said.

"You get to know all the types." He nodded some more. He was a skinny old man with watery blue eyes and yellow teeth. His whole face wrinkled with pleasure at his own remarkable deductive abilities.

"We're shareholders," Alan said.

"That's right," the guard agreed. "Shareholders, Knew it the moment I saw you."

"We'd like to—" Alan started.

"You'd like to take the palace tour—sure, I knew you would. That's what all you shareholders want. Well, next tour leaves in an hour and a half, so in the meantime I suggest you—"

"We don't want the tour," I said.

"Course not." the guard said, with admirable flexibility.

"Tour's a bore. You shareholders have better things to do with your time. You probably want a—"

"We want," Alan said firmly, "to make an appointment with the Comptroller."

That stopped him. His eyes grew narrow, his attitude less cordial.

"Why?"

"Private matters."

He requested our shareholder's cards and we slipped them through the slot in the window. He examined them far longer than necessary. He fed them through a scanner for verification.

"How many shares you own?"

Since I had played my tape of shareholder's rights and privileges many times over during our voyage to Nova Center, I knew that all shareholders were equal regardless of the size of their portfolios. And no shareholder was obligated, under any circumstances besides voting, to divulge the extent of his holdings. So I only said, "A lot."

He didn't press me. He said the Comptroller was a busy man. Rawl-Brook couldn't go having meetings with every shareholder who felt like touching down on Nova Center. So unless it was terribly important . . .

"Who's Rawl-Brook?"

"Who's Rawl-Brook?" The guard snorted. "You want to see the Comptroller and you don't even know who he is!"

"I thought Arel-Spline was—"

"No, Spline hasn't been Comptroller since that traitor Gotz got dethroned."

Alan and I glanced at each other.

"Actually," I said. "it's Spline we want to see. The business we have concerns events which took place during his tenure."

"I'll bet it does! That whole administration was a bunch of thieves. Urtz-Al's cleaned 'em all out, he's put Nova back on her feet. Hail to Urtz-Al!"

This last sentence he spoke quite loudly, looking all around him, hoping, I thought, that somebody might overhear.

"Well, where would we find Arel-Spline?"

"That's not corporate business," the guard said and switched off the intercom.

We stood around the kiosk banging on the window and shouting for attention, but he shook his head and wouldn't reconnect the intercom. Then he started cleaning his nails, pretending we weren't there at all. After a while we walked away, down a path of golden brick edged in bell-shaped flowers, shaded by tall umbrella trees.

"Well, here we are," Alan said, "twenty million light-years from home, on a planet where the one man we're allowed to talk to left three years ago. Terrific."

"Let's look at the bright side. We've got enough money to leave."

"Right. Another twelve thousand CUs. Another month cramped in a space ship. I never should have let you talk me into this."

"Me? Hey, wait a minute. You were the one who wanted to help Gotz, remember?"

"But *you* wanted the yacht to rescue that woman of yours."

"So we're both," I pointed out, "equally responsible."

I thought that finished it. I hoped so, for I was in no mood for quarreling. Then Alan mumbled something.

"What?" I asked.

"I said, you should have talked me out of it."

"Why?"

"Because you're more sensible," he said.

"You know, Alan, there's nothing worse than blaming another for your own stupidity."

"Are you saying I'm stupid?"

I considered the question and replied in the affirmative. That made him really mad. He locked his eyes straight ahead. He set his jaw. His hands, I noticed, made fists at his sides. I stopped, but he kept right on going.

"Alan," I said, "come back here."

He returned, scowling.

"We were *both*," I continued, "equally stupid. We probably shouldn't have come here—but what's done is done, and we might as well make the best of it. This is an interesting planet. We'll spend a few days looking around. Pretend we're tourists."

"What about Ben-Gotz?" Alan said sulkily.

"We'll tell him the truth. That we couldn't find Spline."

"He'll be angry at us."

"So what?"

Alan thought it over. I could see him softening. He said he guessed I was right and he'd try not to complain. Which was good, because I don't know how much longer I could have refrained from kicking him.

Our path wound down into the Valley of the Workers. The

golden bricks gave way to cobblestones, and the bell-shaped flowers were replaced by scraggly weeds. Shacks appeared on either side, wood, stone and scrap metal patched together with wire and spit. The wall of one was a stabilizing fin off a spacecraft, another was built around an old engine cowling. Through the windows, or through holes where windows should have been, I could see folks of every age crowded together, living in unimaginable squalor. Now something peculiar happened. Several families emerged from their shacks and fell into line before and behind us.

More and more came until a parade had formed. A joyless parade it was. The men stared at the ground and dragged their feet. The women were shrewish; each had a passle of whining children clinging to her hem. And several mungpups ran along behind each child, yapping and squealing.

At first I thought they were headed for the factories. The sun was nearing the horizon, and they might have been scheduled for an evening shift. But no, they were too nicely dressed. Their clothes were made of the poorest synthetics, but clean and colorful, clothes for a special occasion.

I turned to ask a stocky fellow trudging alongside me where we were headed. Then I changed my mind—it would have attracted attention. Instead I conferred with Alan and we decided to stay with the crowd and go where it might go. The results were bound to be more interesting than retiring to an inn for the night.

We reached the floor of the valley and crowded down narrow streets lined with teetering hovels which looked as though they might at any moment topple on our heads. The air stank of stews and spices and excrement. The sounds of frightened voices, a fist fight, came from a lixor lobby. A krombar hung from its hind legs in a butcher's stall, flies covering the dark-green carcass. A Scrugal watched us from a second-story window, eyes like stone. And all the while doors were opening yellow in the dusk, people were joining our march. Their shuffling step showed no eagerness—nor could I see reluctance. Simply a mindless mechanical motion.

We turned onto an avenue. Up ahead a silver finger jutted from the ground, listing slightly, drunkenly, like all the other buildings. It was a big old Class C shuttle buried to the top of the tail fins. Painted over the hatch was a five-spoked wheel, and above it:

CHURCH OF THE BODE-SATVA
Welcome One and
All

Alan chuckled. We went inside.

> "I am worker born to suffer,
> Born to toil this sad life long.
> Someone has to weld the steel
> To make the starships fly.
>
> Soon I'll sleep in soft brown dirt
> And let the worms do all the work.
> My soul will sit on the highest peak
> Of Management Hill, of Management Hill."

So they sang as they seated themselves on the cold steel bulkhead. Alan and I found a place near the hatch so we could leave without disturbing anyone if we got bored. After the hymn they dipped their heads three times and, using the index finger, drew circles on their chests, around their hearts.

Now an elevator descended from the bulkhead above and an elfin little man popped out. His head was round and shaven, his eyes were round and bright, his cheeks were round and rosy. Most round of all was his belly, which bobbled beneath his saffron robe as he stepped nimbly to the platform at the far end of the room.

Brother Sava-Nanda—that was his name. He welcomed us one and all, "particularly two happy faces we have not seen before."

The congregation strained their necks to see where he was looking. Alan and I slouched down, trying to make ourselves invisible. To my embarrassment he kept on speaking directly to us. He said that the presence of newcomers was an excellent occasion to recall the story of Bode-Satva. The congregation groaned, as if they had perhaps heard the story of Bode-Satva once too often and would have been happier to go on to other matters. But Brother Sava-Nanda gently ignored them and directed our attention to the walls of the chamber.

On each of the five walls there was a scene from the life of Bode-Satva, painted in a primitive style with lots of color and little regard for perspective. The first showed an infant floating through a ceiling of clouds. Below, all sorts of people gathered awaiting his arrival. They were, according to

Brother Sava-Nanda, kings of industry, great philosophers and Bode-Satva's future parents.

On the second wall Bode-Satva's ma and pa watched with wonder as their teen-aged son chipped away his skin like an eggshell. Beneath was "the magical body which knows neither death or illness, nor suffering of any sort." Wavy lines indicating holy perfection emanated from him.

The third wall gave me a chill. Bode-Satva was an adult. Five men followed him up a ladder of golden ropes. A great jewel hung in the sky above him, just beyond his reach.

"The jewel," Brother Sava-Nanda explained, "is called Lapis. It would have brought salvation to humans everywhere. But alas! Before Bode-Satva and his five disciples could reach it, a terrible war spread across the galaxy!"

The fourth wall depicted that war in grisly detail. The Lapis still hung in the sky, but Bode-Satva was otherwise occupied. Thousands of troops converged on him from every direction. Lightning bolts from each of his fingers struck them dead in their tracks.

"But even Bode-Satva's powers were not without limit."

So it would seem. For in the fifth and last scene he was bound, head, arms and legs, to the five spokes of a wheel, sailing into the fiery center of a star. His feet were burned away, his flesh was singed, his face anguished. A second Bode-Satva sat crosslegged in space watching his own immolation with a peaceful smile.

"Why is he smiling so peaceful? Because Bode-Satva knows that he will return in a new body and recover the Lapis. He will free all humans from suffering. It is very beautiful, yes?"

"I think it's kind of disgusting," Alan whispered, "all that blood . . . "

The congregation began another hymn, but my head was so teeming with ideas, I hardly heard them. That war, could it have been the Great Corporate Revolution of 2412 Ben-Gotz had once spoken of? And was it possible that Bode-Satva and his disciples were the mystical "Wanderer" sect which had been exterminated at the time? Might the Lapis be a human counterpart of the Urs' power stone, a charm to free men from their bodies, to let them travel the golden ropes as I once had? How foolish boundaries of wealth, of birth, of race and ideology would be if men could shed their flesh. And the petty quarreling, the scrapping over money and power and property, how silly it all would seem after a bodiless flight across the universe!

These thoughts led to others, and when my attention finally returned to the present, Brother Sava-Nanda was giving a sermon, something about every worker's responsibility to have as many children as possible.

Then came time for the holy tapes. Before Bode-Satva had died—over four hundred years ago—he had recorded 168,-896 tapes, one to be played each day beginning with the day after his death. Each tape turned to dust after being played, and when no more tapes were left Bode-Satva would return. The tape for the day was #168,781. Less than four months till the day of reckoning. What would Sava-Nanda say when the final tape was played and Bode-Satva did not appear? Then again, maybe he'd show up. It defied reasonable scientific explanation, but the more I saw of this galaxy, the more certain I became that it was vast beyond science or reason.

Brother Sava-Nanda pulled aside the curtain behind him, and there was a vu-screen. He slipped in cassette #168,781 and old Bode-Satva himself filled the screen.

He had a large square jaw, sparkling black eyes and a halo of frizzy hair. He sat on a throne smiling at us, the most serene smile I have ever seen. When he spoke his voice was soft and musical:

> "We are snowflakes.
> Every one of us unique.
> How beautiful!
> Do not mourn the melting,
> The evaporation.
> Again we fall from heaven,
> Again we rise.
> Far more beautiful,
> Don't you think?
> Om Shanti."

Then the tape was over and Brother Sava-Nanda pulled the cassette from the machine. He held it up in his left hand, bowed his head three times and circled his heart with his right index finger. The tape went *spouff*! Then his hand was empty and a cloud of fine white dust was drifting toward the vent.

"Even the word of Bode-Satva," Brother Sava-Nanda said, "is transient."

I found this deeply moving, but those around me had not been similarly affected. Many of them were asleep. Others were whispering, local gossip. The children ran through the aisles chasing the mungpups, teasing them and tugging their tails. All of them snapped to attention when Brother Sava-Nanda announced: "Time for the sacrament!" The sleepers woke, the whisperers fell silent, the children turned to cherubs. They formed a line and passed by the platform with their mouths open. Brother Sava-Nanda placed several drops from a bottle of grayish liquid on each outstuck tongue. This, he explained, was Bode-Satva's spittle.

Well, whatever Bode-Satva had in his spittle, it affected the congregation more than all his tapes and tales put together. They left the platform giggling, scarcely able to keep their balance. Their eyes turned vague and distant. Some collapsed on the cold steel bulkhead and lay there laughing, squirming with sensual pleasure.

6

"Fascinating," Alan remarked later, "how that little church has managed to survive by adapting to UltraCap."

We were wandering down a cobblestone street, savoring the fresh night air, looking for an inn where we might bed down.

"Management Hill," he continued, "tolerates them because they encourage the workers to procreate, and keep them docile with promises of salvation. And the workers keep coming back for that spittle—some kind of euphoriant, don't you think? Meanwhile they manage to get their doctrine across, a sugar-coated pill. Very clever." We walked a little farther and he added, "But what a lot of borselshit!"

"Oh, I don't know," I said.

"You don't believe there's any truth to it?"

"There's truth to everything," I said, "but often it's well hidden, and you have to dig very deep to get at it."

7

As chance would have it, the first inn we came to was the White Dwarf. It looked no worse than any of the other hovels, and breakfast and bed were only fourteen CUs. Included in the price were the services of a cute chambermaid, Je-Nett, who kept us up most of the night demonstrating scruing positions. Many were local favorites I had never seen before, for example, "Refueling in Orbit." (The male ship extends his hose while the female rotates slowly, scratching his fuel tanks.)

Next morning we dressed and breakfasted and went out in the sunshine, intending to enjoy ourselves as if we were tourists on a holiday. But the thought of Ben-Gotz waiting in New Panama cast a pall over everything. We were, after all, his only hope.

The streets were empty, except for a few mungpups scrounging in the garbage, and most of the shops were closed. Nearly everyone had gone to the factories. Presently we saw a store that was open, a souvenir shop. The window was filled with mugs and ashtrays and plates and satchels and caftans, all decorated with scenes of Nova Center. Alan, however, was more intrigued by the toy spacecraft.

"I used to build those when I was a kid," he said, pressing against the window. "Spent weeks gluing all the little parts together, seeing how neatly I could paint them. But I'll tell you something, even when I was eight years old I built better spaceships than those."

He was right. They were the worst-looking spaceships I'd ever seen. Parts glued on wrong, decals peeling, sloppy paint jobs.

We pushed open the door and some little bells jingled. A thin voice from the back called, "Yes?"

"Just looking," I said, and thumbed through a rack of picture post-tapes.

Alan inspected some toy spaceships spread on the counter, making little noises of disapproval.

We wandered into the back of the store and there was the proprietor bent over a table, gluing together a toy spaceship by the light of one dim bulb, and making an awful mess of it.

"Hi," Alan said.

"Hello." The proprietor didn't look up.

"You know," Alan said, "that's a lot easier if you use tweezers. And you can wipe the excess glue away with a little piece of rag. No—that's the top of the breeder pile, it goes on the side of the—"

"*I don't care!*"

The spaceship shattered against the wall and the proprietor buried his head in his arms and started to cry.

"Oh gee, I'm sorry," Alan said. "I was just trying to help. You were doing pretty well—"

"No I wasn't . . . I wasn't . . . I can't build these stupid things . . . oh, what am I doing here? What am I doing here?"

Alan rushed around the room. He found a carafe of lixor on a shelf, a plastic flask decorated with a scene of the Executive Palace, and poured a cup.

"Here, drink this," he said, patting the proprietor on the back.

The proprietor sipped and sniffed. Then he burst into tears again.

Alan brought him a handkerchief embroidered with a scene of the Ford River Refineries belching smoke.

The proprietor honked a few times and wiped his eyes, which were quite red. He smiled at us sheepishly.

"I must apologize. Sometimes . . . the strain of what I've been through . . . and gluing together all those tiny pieces . . ."

Then, before I could stop him, Alan volunteered to build a few ships for him. That way he could see how it was done. Good old Alan. We'd be spending the rest of the week in that half-lit room ruining our eyes, asphyxiating ourselves with glue.

But the proprietor was beside himself with gratitude. He pumped our hands. He offered us lixor. He introduced himself. His name was Arel-Spline.

"The Comptroller?"

"The *ex*-Comptroller. Ever since dear Ben-Gotz—" He stopped himself and looked around nervously. He shouted, "Hail to Urtz-Al!"

"You don't have to do that," I said. "Ben-Gotz sent us."

Arel Spline's eyes opened wide. He looked at me and he looked at Alan, and he looked at me again.

I don't think he was much past forty-five, but he appeared older, hunched from bending over his work table, squinty from staring in the poor light. Deep lines traversed his forehead, ringed his eyes and fell on either side of his nose. His complexion was sallow, his hair was white. His nostrils were mysterious caves.

"Hail to Urtz-Al," he repeated with less conviction.

"Gotz sent us. Honest. He's alive and he needs your help."

"Ben-Gotz is an embezzler. Lower than the lowliest drak." This he said with such little conviction that only a deaf man would have been fooled. Hesitantly, he continued, "It's not really true, is it? Ben-Gotz, alive ... if you're lying to me, you're horribly cruel." Tears slipped down the twin grooves of his nose. "Dear Ben-Gotz ... noble Ben-Gotz ..."

I'd never seen a man with such overdeveloped irrigational facilities. When his supply of tears was finally exhausted we sat down together and told him all that Ben-Gotz had told us.

"I knew he was innocent," Spline sniffled. "I knew it all along. We three will restore him to the throne. Justice will be done!"

"So you think the recorder wasn't discovered? And the yacht wasn't destroyed?"

"Well, I haven't seen it since Urtz-Al took the throne. A man named Ammen-Jub used to pilot it. Now he's master of the palace landing pad—that must have been his reward for betraying our beloved president. We'll corner him tonight at the White Dwarf ... roast him with lasar light till he tells us where the yacht is. If he won't talk we'll burn a hole in his face. By the time we're done death will be a pleasure."

"Couldn't we just offer him a bribe?" Alan asked timidly.

But it was clear from Spline's expression that the cruelest torture would be too kind for any betrayer of Ben-Gotz.

8

The tables at the White Dwarf were surplus hatch covers of the hardest steel; yet someone had scratched in the surface, *J-M A WORKER BORN TO TOIL*. I ran my fingers over the crude letters and imagined J-M, whoever he was, scraping away with a pocket knife or maybe just a shard of glass, night after night. What determination it must have taken! What tenacity, to leave this little momento of his existence, this shred of immortality! Once, I remember learning in school, men had written whole *books*, hundreds and hundreds of pages handlettered so that they might be remembered after death. The human animal is, I think, quite glorious on occasion.

Arel-Spline interrupted my reverie. He leaned across the table and whispered, "That's him."

Through the sea of blue cigar smoke I could make out seven men at the bar. They drank a bubbly lixor called Flitch from big mugs, tilting back their heads and pouring it straight down their throats. In between swallows their raucous talk filled the room.

"The last one on the left."

They were big men all of them, but the one Spline pointed to was the biggest of all. His hair was cropped almost to the skull and his neck was nearly as thick as his head. The sleeves of his coveralls had been cut away to expose massive, sinewy arms. He wore a thick brass band around either wrist and a stinger strapped across his chest. He turned his cold blue eyes in my direction and I looked away immediately.

"What are you waiting for?" Arel-Spline asked. "Go get him!"

"Are you kidding?" Alan said. "Go get him yourself."

"I would," Spline demurred, "if it wasn't for my back. Now, ten years ago I wouldn't have thought twice about—"

"Look," I said, "force is out of the question. He's got fifty pounds on any of us—plus a stinger."

"You have another way?" Spline asked.

Actually, my mind was a blank. All I could think about was his huge hands cracking my head like a chicklenut.

Then I noticed Je-Nett, the chambermaid who had been so instructive last night. She was coming down the stairs with a tray of dirty plates and mugs. Her breasts were half-exposed—her dress lifted and shaped them like shuttle ships in their cradles—and as she passed the bar Ammen-Jub came up behind her and put his hands over them. She blushed prettily and laughed and caught him in the ribs with the side of the tray without upsetting a single dish. He grimaced with pain, yet the rejection had been performed with such charm and grace he could not be angry. Clearly Je-Nett was as skilled at avoiding men as she was at pleasing them.

She continued on her way, and when she passed our table I called her name. She grinned to see us, her cheeks making dimples. A missing front tooth reminded me of an open door.

"God, my feet . . ." she moaned, dropping into the chair next to mine. "First break I've had all evening. I can only stay a minute or the boss will start screaming." She sighed with exhaustion. "What a life! All day on my feet, all night on my back. Bad enough being born a worker, worse being born a woman. Worst of all being born red." She shook back the thick copper hair that hung to her shoulders. Her skin was freckled with cinnamon. "It's the passion-color, see? That's why I can't help myself with pretty boys like you." She laughed. "Enough complaining. How are my lovelies?"

"We've got a problem," I said. "The man at the bar—Ammen-Jub's his name?"

"Oh, I know him well—I can't pass him without a hand grabbing my bosom. It's one thing when men are gentle and considerate and make a lady feel like she's got a say in the matter. But fellows like him—well, I'd give him a sharp one in the fueling spheres if I had a chance."

Alan was grinning ear to ear, and I felt the same. There's nothing as flattering as being favorably compared to a man who's half a head taller than you. Particularly if you're short, as I am. My ego was swelled to the bursting point—so was my member—and I would have taken her right there on the table if not for my duty to Ben-Gotz.

"Would he go upstairs with you," I asked, "if he had the chance?"

"Would he!" She laughed. "In a minute. But he won't if I can help it."

"What about for a hundred CUs?"

"I'm no Scrugal."

"All you'd have to do is get him upstairs and undressed. Make sure he's far away from his stinger. Then we'll take over."

She raised an eyebrow. "And I thought you were nice boys. Shows what a fine judge of character I am. One hundred CUs, eh?"

I nodded.

"In advance?"

I peeled off the bills. She slipped them into the deep valley between her breasts.

"Room three," she said, "in five minutes."

Then she rose from the table, very businesslike, picked up her tray and started back toward the bar.

This time when Ammen-Jub grabbed her from behind she let his hands stay. She pressed back against him, wriggling her behind. Well, the look on his face was something to see! He'd grown so accustomed to her rebuffs that this change in behavior left him stymied. She whispered something in his ear and started up the steps. A few seconds—then he broke into a broad grin. He rubbed his hands together like somebody sitting down to a five-course dinner and bounded after her, three steps at a time.

Five minutes later we followed too. Up the steps, then a dark hallway. Eight doors, eight rooms for lodgers. I put my ear to number three. Sounds of scuffling, of panting breath.

"No!—wait a minute, please!" (That was Je-Nett.)

"I've got to take off my . . ."

Ripping cloth.

"All right," I whispered. "At the count of three. Alan and I will take on Jub. Arel-Spline, you'll grab the stinger and cover us. Move fast as you can—surprise is our advantage. Ready? One . . . two . . ."

"Three!"

I threw my weight against the door and we tumbled inside. But I hadn't counted on Jub's preference for doing it in the dark. The shades were drawn, the lights were out. Couldn't see a thing. I rushed forward, swinging my bionic hand like a club. Something caught me in the shins and I tripped into a tangle of bodies and bedsheets and thrashing limbs. Were there really only five of us in the room? I felt as if I were fighting off an army! I started twisting an arm and Je-Nett cried, "It's *me*, you fool!" Then somebody grabbed me from

behind and threw me against the wall. I groped my way back
to the bed. My hands found a thick neck and I squeezed with
all my might. Another pair of hands closed around my neck,
but I gave a kick backward and freed myself without losing
my hold. Then a crash, a dull thud, a groan.

The lights went on. Je-Nett had a finger on the light switch
and her other hand wrapped around the stinger. She was aim-
ing it at Ammen-Jub, who lay at her feet—both of them were
stark naked. As for the neck I was squeezing with such gusto,
it belonged to poor Arel-Spline—as if he hadn't suffered
enough already! His face was purple and his tongue was
hanging out. I let go instantly and started to apologize, but he
was gasping so hard I don't think he heard. And Alan was lying on the floor, rubbing a lump the size of a brinko fruit
that had grown out of his forehead. So things had not gone
exactly according to plan. Still, Jub was where I wanted him.

Je-Nett handed me the stinger. "He's all yours," she said.

"Nice work," I said.

"No thanks to you. You're the clumsiest thieves I've seen
in my life. It's a wonder you've lived this long."

"My CUs," Ammen-Jub said, "are in the top pocket of my
coveralls. Take them and be done with it."

"That's not what I'm after," I said. "Where's Ben-Gotz's
yacht?"

"How should I know?" Jub's eyes were hard as slate.

"You know because you betrayed him. You abandoned
him on Junglabesh."

I thought I saw a flicker of a reaction.

"Not me, friend. You've got the wrong man. But if you
take that stinger away from my head I'll forget about this
little indignity. So long as I never see your face again on
Nova Center."

"He's lying," Spline rasped. The red memory of my fingers
on his neck made me feel awful. "You piloted the yacht back
without Gotz. Admit it!"

"I admit it. Gotz found out that Urtz-Al knew he was an
embezzler and suicided. I saw him do it. He walked out an
airlock and deep-froze himself."

"I spoke with Gotz," I said, "two months ago."

Now I did very definitely see a reaction. Encouraged, I
forced the barrel of the stinger into his mouth and tightened
my finger around the trigger.

"You have five seconds," I said, "to tell me what happened
to Gotz's yacht."

"The Sargasso Sea! We left it in the Sargasso Sea."

"What's that?"

"A junkyard." He spoke quickly now. "Nova dumps her salvage there—the old ships and the test designs that didn't work out."

"Where is it?"

"I'll give you the coordinates. There's a pen and paper in my coveralls."

"Stay where you are. Je-Nett, get it for him."

He wrote down a series of numbers and I noticed that he hesitated before writing down the last. When he handed me the paper I looked it over, but it meant nothing to me. What did I know about navigational coordinates? He could have written down his ID number and I'd have been none the wiser.

"Ben-Gotz," I said, "is coming back to take the throne. If these coordinates are correct—*if* we locate the yacht—I'll see to it that you're promoted. If they're wrong you'll be liquidated. Understand?"

"Give me the paper." He changed the last digit and handed it back.

"Likewise, if you breathe a word of what happened here tonight—immediate liquidation. Understand?"

He nodded.

"Also," I continued, "you keep your hands off Je-Nett unless she tells you otherwise."

He nodded. But I could see that bothered him more than the rest combined.

9

Alan and I were in our room packing when we heard footsteps outside the door. I grabbed the stinger I'd borrowed from Ammen-Jub and moved to one side where I wouldn't be seen. Alan prepared to answer it.

"Who's there?"

"It's me." Je-Nett's voice.

We relaxed and let her in.

"You clowns," she said affectionately, "you really loused things up."

"We got what we wanted," I said.

"You also got me fired. The boss said I had no business making customers when I should have been making beds."

"How dare he!" Alan said. He was outraged. "I'm going down there right now and change his mind.

He marched for the door and she stopped him with an arm around the waist and gave him a hug.

"You're a dear—but I don't want my job back."

"If," I offered, "there's something else we can do . . ."

"Take me with you."

"To the Sargasso Sea?"

"Please! I can help. My father runs a servicedome on an asteroid at the outskirts of the sea. I haven't seen him in nine years—and I miss him so! He'll help you recover the yacht. He knows the area like the back of his hand and he's got all kinds of salvage equipment. Oh please. Please take me with you."

Before I could protest, Alan had agreed. And afterward we were so deluged with kisses and caresses, well, I just didn't have the heart.

Next morning we called the Nova spaceport. They put us in touch with a shuttle service that would take us to Je-Nett's father's asteroid for a reasonable fee. I booked three seats on a noon liftoff.

She needed a few hours to pack and say goodbye to friends. Meanwhile Alan and I strolled over to Arel-Spline's souvenir shop to tell him we were on our way and not to give up hope. No need for our reassurance, it turned out. He was in the back of the shop, preening before a mirror, wearing a green uniform with gold braid and a number of medals pinned to the breast. "My old Comptroller's uniform," he explained and proudly showed us how well it still fit.

We left him admiring himself and wandered the winding streets until, quite by accident, we came upon the Church of Bode-Satva. Brother Sava-Nanda and six other little men were digging next to the mound of dirt which covered the base of the ship, a hole some six feet deep by ten feet wide. We strolled over to the edge to watch them work.

No auto-shovels for these folks—they dug with antique spades, pushing them into the earth with sandaled feet, scooping the dirt into buckets, then carrying the buckets up a ladder and dumping them on the mound. The sleeves of their saffron robes were rolled to the shoulder and I was surprised by the size of their biceps. On a hot day like this I was glad to be a watcher instead of a digger.

Presently Brother Sava-Nanda noticed us. He stuck his spade in the ground and called up to us:

"Ah! Two happy faces from off world! Om-Shanti!"

"Hello," I said. "What are you doing?"

"Digging a hole," he called back.

Well, I could see that. "Why?"

"Last night we play Holy Tape #168,783. Everybody joyfully, surprised! Bode-Satva say:

> " 'Auspicious moments!
> When stars and planets are favorably aligned,
> When we come to knots in the ropes of time.
> When high tide lets us launch endeavors
> Otherwise run aground. . . .
>
> The moment of man's fate draws near,
> That is to say, the day of my return.
> Prepare, oh dearest brothers.
> Dig into the earth where I am buried
> Like a precious jewel.
> Om Shanti.' "

He dipped his head three times and circled his heart with his index finger.

Alan cleared his throat. "That tape," he said. "It was recorded a long time ago?"

"Four hundred and sixty years ago," Sava-Nanda agreed, with a broad grin—he never stopped grinning.

"Was Bode-Satva *on* this planet when he recorded it?"

Brother Sava-Nanda scratched his head and gazed at the sky. "No, he was on the planet Putta in the star system Parthe."

"Well, then," Alan continued delicately, "assuming the tape isn't metaphorical . . ."

"No metaphor! Bode-Satva speaks only the truth!"

"All right, it's not metaphor, but don't you think he meant to dig there, on *that* planet?"

"Oh no," Sava-Nanda shook his head. "Bode-Satva is the Jivan-Mukta, the master magician. He lives outside the lie of time, so all past and future is open to his eyes. He knew where we would be, and he will know where we have been. No more talk now, back to digging. Om Shanti."

And he picked up his spade and went back to work.

"Oh to have such faith," Alan said, as we walked back to the White Dwarf. "What a pleasure life must be."

Part V

The Sargasso Sea

1

I knew something was wrong from the moment we landed at the service dome and I saw Je-Nett's father in the lavatory, polishing the toilet bowl as if it were some precious antique. His hair was gray and matted like a bird's nest and his beard was caked with drool. His skin was white and wrinkly, almost transparent with purple veins pulsing in his temples. He wore coveralls of shiny yellow fabric crimped with green elastic at the wrists and ankles, and by a green utility belt at the waist. Embroidered across his chest in florid script: *Ar-Nett's Service Station*—a flashy outfit but ripped at the seams and smeared with dirt and oil. Yes, I knew something was wrong but I blocked it from my mind and said nothing, for Alan had committed us, and commitments, as I see it, once made must be honored. Otherwise all human dealings shred like tissue.

The old man rose and brushed off his knees and said, "Clean restrooms and good food, that's what keeps the spacers coming."

Well, the floor of the service dome was inch-deep in dust. Overhead lights were burned out and the plastic countertop peeled in curls like sun-baked skin. Furthermore, the life-support systems were clanking and groaning like a team of tortured ghosts, and I feared that at any moment the noise might cease, subjecting us to a drop in temperature, a loss of pressure and a most slow and ghastly death.

Je-Nett ran over to her father and hugged him and lay her head against his breast.

"Where have you been?" he asked. "It's almost time for supper."

"I went to Nova Center, Daddy. Don't you remember?"

He looked at the ceiling for a minute.

"You went away with that worthless spacer?"

"Yes, Daddy, but I'm back now."

I knew what they were talking about. Je-Nett had told us

the whole story during passage. For years she and her father had run the service dome all by themselves—her mother died when she was a little girl—assisted only by a utility robot named Joe. Business had been good. A warp-route folded near them and ships emerging from months in space would shuttle down to their tiny asteroid to consult with Ar-Nett, whose reputation as an aerospace engineer was known across the galaxy. (At least that's what Je-Nett said. But I imagine the men probably needed servicing more than their machines, and Je-Nett herself was the main attraction.)

Then the warp-route had vanished as warp-routes do, suddenly, without cause or reason, and with it had gone their trade. Since they happened to be located at the edge of the Sargasso Sea, garbage scows and junkers still touched down occasionally. But for the most part it was a routine of unimaginable boredom. So when a handsome spacer, a test pilot for Nova, offered to take Je-Nett away—well, who could blame her for accepting?

"Daddy, these are my friends, Alan-Tal and Stefin-Dae."

"Spacers?" he asked, looking us up and down.

"No, Daddy, they're good solid citizens. Shareholders."

"Shareholders!" The old man seemed pleased. "I don't like spacers coming around and giving my little girl ideas. Makes her discontent. We've got a good life here. Safe and secure. Out there"—he waved toward the infinite beyond the eggshell dome—"a person doesn't know what's going to happen."

"Daddy, where's Joe?"

"That old tin can? Probably sitting in a hole somewhere, diddling his servos. Honey, why don't you fix us some supper? Make those fritters you made last week."

"Last week?" Alan whispered.

I shrugged.

Je-Nett went behind the counter and started taking out pans and tubes of nutrients, raising small dust storms with every motion.

"Best cook in the star system," Ar-Nett told us confidentially. "Good food and clean restrooms, that's what keeps them coming. So you fellows are shareholders? How about that! What are you doing way out here?"

"Salvage work," I said. "Je-Nett told us you were pretty good."

"Pretty good? I don't mean to brag, sonny, but if you're talking about fishing in the Sargasso Sea, well, I'm about the best there is."

He smiled and nodded and suddenly lost his balance, grabbing the edge of the counter, clinging to it for several seconds, his face filled with fear. Then it passed. He straightened. He smiled and continued as if nothing had happened.

"What're you fishing for, sonny? A good breeder? An antimatter bottle? Or maybe some precious cargo? I'm warning you, you may be wasting your time. Most of those ships have been picked clean to the bone."

He was interrupted by the airlock chimes. The double doors at the other end of the room slid open and a robot entered. At least I think it was a robot. Hard to say. One of the eyes was cracked, the chest was dented, fingers were missing from both hands, and the legs were bent out of shape. It wobbled into the room going "Bleep-*urgh*, bleep-*urgh*, bleep-*urgh*, bleep-*urgh*."

Je-Nett called to it: "Joe!"

The robot's head revolved forty-five degrees, joints squeaking to raise the hairs on your neck. Within its face lights flashed and it went *erk! erk! erk!* Then a voice came creaking with static from its speaker.

"Miss Je-Nett welcome back I have missed you."

She put her arms around its wide torso, and kissed its speaker.

"Oh, Joe, I missed you too!"

"Hey, you lazy bag of bolts," Ar-Nett shouted from the lavatory, where he was now scrubbing the sink. "Help Je-Nett with supper, you miserable rust-trap."

So Joe followed her behind the counter, put on an apron and started tearing up lettuce paper for a salad.

He had been at it no more than a minute when the clatter of the life-support systems underwent a subtle change. A siren sounded.

"Excuse me," Joe crackled, wobbling toward the airlock. "The oxygen reclamation system has broken down again I will return shortly."

"Never a dull moment," I told Je-Nett, who was calmly shaping nutrients into patties.

"Poor Joe," she said. "He's always repairing the machinery. And Daddy thinks he's just sitting around recharging his cells. He calls Joe all kind of names. But Joe never complains."

"About your father," I said carefully. "Is he all right?"

"Certainly."

"Oh. I was wondering, the way he's scrubbing the bathroom."

"*All* engineers are meticulous. I guess Daddy gets a little carried away, though."

"I guess." I ran a finger over the countertop and stared at the stripe I'd made in the dust.

"He doesn't seem to remember that you went away," Alan said.

"Well, he's getting old. His memory's not what it should be."

She continued, "He'll salvage your yacht, if that's what you're worried about. He may have some funny habits, but Daddy's an expert. He's the best there is."

2

We cleared the dust off the floor and arranged some foam cushions into a bed. Ar-Nett had offered us a choice of guest rooms in the secondary dome. But after the old man had gone to bed, Joe wobbled in and advised against it.

"The secondary dome is in disrepair I could make it habitable perhaps but it would not be safe better sleep here."

"Joe," I said, "you're a terrific robot—you keep the station running singlehanded. I know you love Je-Nett and anybody can see how loyal you are to her dad. But tomorrow we're going to be putting our future in his hands and we've got to know how . . . *reliable* he is."

"Reliable?"

"You know what I mean. His state of mind. His sanity."

Joe hesitated a long time. Things went *click-i-ty*, *click-i-ty*, *click-i-ty* inside him and other things went *wreeeeeeee*. Presently his speaker crackled:

"Ar-Nett invested everything in this station for a time business was good. Then there was no business and I told Ar-Nett to give up the station and start a new life but he would not listen because I am a machine and what do machines know? We stay and I try to keep everything running I try to keep everything repaired I have conversations with Ar-Nett so his mind will stay active. But I am only one machine I am afraid that I have failed Ar-Nett's mind is not in good condition."

"It's all right," I said. "Nobody's blaming you."

"You ask about sanity I define sanity as the ability to differentiate between empirical reality and illusion as the ability to function in societal context. Note the following symptoms: (A) superstition example belief that clean restrooms and good food will bring customers despite evidence to contrary; (B) paranoia example fear spacers try to divest him of livelihood again counter reality; (C) disorientation in time/space example falling sensations loss of memory general confusion."

"But aside from that he's fine?" I asked.

"Men joke in face of fear I understand but this is not funny according to my definition humor. Chance for Ar-Nett to engage in goal-oriented task with human companionship such as yacht-salvage program you propose is beneficial for ego already positive results have been observed suggest you proceed."

"Don't worry, Joe," Alan chirped, "we will. We're going to help that old guy back to health. Maybe we can even figure out a way to bring some customers out here, drum up a little business."

"For God's sake, Alan, stop it! You go around making promises to everybody and every time you do we're in it deeper and deeper. How do you expect to help others when you can't even help yourself?"

"Oh I can't help myself, huh? Well, it seems to me I've been doing pretty well since I left the AUAR. The only big mistake I made was going along with you on this stupid trip, that's how it seems to me. Instead of criticizing everybody and being so damned superior, why don't you try and . . ."

We could have gone on with it all night, but then Je-Nett appeared—she had been saying goodnight to her father—wearing a silky green nightdress which set off the cinnamon skin. And there on the foam pillows, on the dusty dome floor, in time to the crippled tympanum of the life-support system beating like a heart with a faulty valve, she reconciled all our differences.

Ar-Nett's salvage machine—Betsy, he called it—looked more like a surface vehicle than an airship. It was a squat box sixty feet long with caterpillar treads and a bubble on top which afforded the operator an unimpaired view, 360 degrees. Six old-fashioned liquid-fueled rockets mounted on the outside swiveled to supply vertical or horizontal thrust as needed. These were more than sufficient to escape the asteroid's minimal gravity and more efficient than fusion engines for short jaunts and fine maneuvers. Two mechanical "hands"—they looked more like lobsopper claws—could be extended from the front to perform delicate operations in space without the operator having to leave the vehicle. All in all it looked like an efficient little machine, ideally suited for our needs, and I said so.

Ar-Nett, who had customized it himself, beamed with pride.

Perhaps Joe was right, perhaps this job would help his mental condition. Already that morning Ar-Nett had shaven the dreadful tangle off his chin and made an attempt to comb his hair. And his stench wasn't as bad as the day before, either. From my own experience I know that reclusiveness is the finest breeder of delusion, while working with others, *meaningful* work—what little there is of it—brings sanity and well-being.

Je-Nett gave us a basket of fried chickett which she and Joe had spent the morning preparing. They wished us love and luck as we passed through the special airlock which led directly into Betsy's hull.

Talk about claustrophobia. We were none of us big men, but every time I turned I smacked Alan with my elbow or bumped heads with Ar-Nett. Functional Betsy left only a small space for passengers; the rest of her was crammed with spacesuits and power lasers, test equipment and diagnostic computers. It seemed a little bigger once Ar-Nett had climbed up into the bubble.

"Here we go!" he shouted. And the ship shook a little, but that was all.

"Thatta way, Betsy, thatsa girl—easy does it, now, come up easy—now show 'em your stuff!"

He might have been taming a wild borsel.

Later he unbuckled and swam down to join us, hardly touching the handholds. You can always tell how experienced a man is in space by the way he moves in zero G. I began to feel secure.

"I gave Betsy the coordinates," he said, meaning those we had pried from Ammen-Jub, "and she thinks it'll be seven or eight hours, so we might as well settle back and enjoy ourselves. Want a stick of gum?"

It was appleloupe flavor, the kind that tastes stronger the more you chew.

"I don't feel right," he continued, "unless I'm out in space. Gravity makes me logy. I'm a space babe through and through. Know what I'm planning to do? Open my own service station. I heard a new warp-route unfolded near Nova Center. If I could find an asteroid in the neighborhood, think of the business I'd do! A million ships a year pass through there. We'd have a restaurant—my wife's a hell of a cook—and rooms where spacers could put up, and maybe even a—"

"Excuse me," Alan said. "Your wife?"

"Laura. Never met Laura? I've got her picture here."

He took a hollo-ball out of a storage chest, wiped it off on his sleeve and handed it to me. I squeezed it and in the middle of the ball a head appeared, a red-haired woman.

"That's Je-Nett," I said.

Ar-Nett laughed. "No, no. In twenty years, maybe. Je-Nett's just learning to toddle." He snapped his fingers and groaned. "It's her birthday—she's one year old and I forgot completely! Laura's going to give it to me."

"Ar-Nett," Alan said slowly, "how can she be one year old? You must be seventy."

"Who, me? I'm thirty-four and the ladies tell me I might as well be twenty."

"Look at yourself—look at your hands."

"My hands?"

He turned them slowly in front of his face, the tissue-paper skin, the throbbing blue veins.

"My hands! No . . ."

He regarded us with fear and confusion. Then, mumbling something about checking the course, he swam back up to the bubble.

"Why'd I do that?" Alan whispered. "I feel like shit."

So did I; as though I had robbed him of forty years of life, even though his own broken mind was the thief.

We sat there feeling miserable for three hours, but Ar-Nett recovered quickly enough. He swam down again, smiling.

"What do you say we break open the lunch basket? My little girl makes the best fried chickett this side of Hebres Gamma."

"Your little girl?" Alan tested, cautiously.

"Je-Nett—you forget about her that quick? I think you boys must be amnesiac. Or senile, ha-ha-ha!"

Far be it from me, after all the synthetic garbage I've eaten, to consider myself an expert judge of food. Maybe Je-Nett did make good fried chickett—I didn't even know what chickett was—but it tasted like poison. I suppressed a gag, fearing I'd offend Ar-Nett. Alan, however, retched rather loudly and spit the food into his hand.

"What's the trouble?" Ar-Nett asked.

"Something in the food," Alan asked.

"Loving care," the old man replied. "Finest ingredient in the galaxy."

"Uh-uh. Something else."

"You silky-stomached shareholders don't know good food from plastic."

Alan took another nibble, rolling it around in his mouth. "Very familiar." He closed his eyes. Then he popped them open. "I know! Psychomimetimine-D."

"What's that?" I asked.

"A drug. We used to take it in college, for fun. It makes you cra—"

He stopped short. He stared at the chickett. He stared at Ar-Nett. He said:

"Do me a favor? Don't eat any more."

"Why the hell not?"

"Because I think there was an accident and some chemicals got in the food."

"You're nuts," Ar-Nett snorted. "I won't let this good cooking go to waste."

He reached for another piece of chickett, but Alan

snatched it away and carried the basket back to the lavatory. I heard the toilet flush. He came back with the basket empty.

"You crazy fool," Ar-Nett cried. "Why'd you go and do that?"

Alan just shook his head.

"Of all the fool things. What'll we eat?"

"You've got emergency rations," I said, "don't you?"

"Yes, but . . . aw, what's the use. You kids are crazy."

"Hey," I whispered, when Ar-Nett was back in the bubble, "you don't really think the drug got in there by accident?"

"What do you think, Stefin? He's so used to the taste he doesn't notice it. Somebody's been slipping it in his food for years."

"But, who . . . ?" I started to ask before I realized who it had to be.

4

Ar-Nett called us. We squeezed into the bubble with him and I gasped.

"Isn't that a sight," he said, his voice soft with wonder. "I've been here a million times and I still get the chills."

I had the impression of moving through some labyrinthine crypt, the geometric carcasses of ships stacked on all sides, ships of every size and shape, eaten by time, bound by what appeared to be giant spiderwebs, and stippled with space barnacles.

Ar-Nett spoke in hushed tones, as if in respect for the dead.

"We should be there any minute. It's a yacht, you say?"

I nodded. "A fancy one. It belonged to the Prez of Nova."

A giant ship, an arrangement of spheres and cylinders linked by a latticework of beams, was rushing toward us. I ducked my head instinctively as it swept past the bubble.

"Just missed you," Ar-Nett said, "by eighty-one miles."

I apologized. "Hard to judge distance out here."

"Sure is, sonny."

A blip appeared at the edge of the vu-screen. Ar-Nett started pulling levers and pushing buttons and working the foot pedals like some mad organist. The blip drifted toward the "O" coordinates of the cross-hairs.

"I believe that's your prize. We'll have visual identification in a minute."

Alan whistled.

A ship had appeared dead ahead, an exquisite silver fish trapped in a web of filaments. It grew quickly at first, then slower as Ar-Nett cut our speed. Finally it stopped, close enough to read the lettering over the wing.

NOVA 1.

"She's a beauty all right," Ar-Nett mused. "And it looks like she's in good shape. Must have a spanium hull. Problem is, she's a little *too* pretty. Quizzles like those shiny ones. Got her all tied up."

"You mean those cables?" Alan asked. "They're not man-made?"

"No sir. Quizzles spin 'em."

"Quizzles? What's a quizzle?"

"It's a lump of rock," Ar-Nett explained, "that thinks it's an animal. They wander between the stars looking for energy, any kind of energy at all. Nuclear fuel, pulsar radiation, even *prana*—human energy. That's a special delicacy. Strange kind of creature. Some scientists say it's them unfold the warp-routes, but nobody's proved it. No, I don't like the looks of that web. You boys ever do any extravehicular activity? No? Well, it's a good time to learn."

"You want us to go out there?" Alan asked in disbelief.

"Somebody's got to cut those cables."

"What about the mechanical hands?"

"The waldos? We'd be here for months. You boys go out there with power lasers, you'll have the job done in an hour."

"What if—what if the quizzles come around?"

"Not much chance. There's thousands of ships and only a handful of quizzles. In all my years I've only seen two."

"I can't go," Alan continued with increasing desperation. He held out his palms to me. "Stefin, reason with him."

I hated to let Alan down, but the idea of an EVA tickled me; a chance to leave the ship, to swim through starry space with only a thin suit separating me from the eternal spirit.

"Let's go put on the pressure suits," I said.

"I am," Alan said, "the only sane one left."

Maybe he was right.

5

We emerged like soap bubbles from the airlock. A short burst from our jet packs propelled us across the abyss between the two ships. It was like nothing else I'd ever experienced, drifting without weight or substance through the silent void. My second skin was stuffy, stiff-jointed, green-faceplated to dim the dazzling stars. I wished the floating would go on forever—then *clank*, my magnetic boots yanked me to Gotz's yacht, like being slapped out of a reverie. Alan arrived a few feet away. I clunked my glove against his helmet and pointed "up." Betsy was hanging upside down some forty feet overhead—I could even see Ar-Nett inside the operator's bubble, like a tiny doll.

"Look," I called to Alan over the radio, "there's Ar-Nett."

"Yeah," Alan said weakly. "Please, let's get this over with."

We walked, like lead-footed men, along the top of the yacht until we came to the place where the filaments girdled her, gray grainy cables about the thickness of my finger. I turned on the power laser and lowered the protective visor over my faceplate. Then I aimed the beam, a needle of white light, at a cable and held it steady there. Soon the cable frayed. It snapped and the end whipped about as if it were alive, spinning around the hull unraveling itself. Freed, it vanished into the darkness, or so it appeared.

I went to work on the other cables and they too gave easily. Twenty minutes later only one remained. Now I noticed that, without the other cables to counteract it, the remaining one was gradually pulling us away from Betsy. I went to work on it, speaking to Ar-Nett at the same time through my helmet radio.

"Hello—we're drifting away from you. Can you move Betsy up a little closer? I'm afraid we'll lose you."

Ar-Nett's voice came back, "Sorry, Va-Deem, it's my little girl's birthday—Je-Nett's one year old today—and I've got to get back to base and send her a message. A man's family comes first.

"*Ar-Nett*," Alan screamed. "*Don't go—you can send her a message later! Please . . .*"

Betsy rotated away from us. She began to diminish in size.

"*Ar-Nett, don't go, please, for God's sake come back!*"

Alan ran along the hull, arduously lifting the magnetic boots—a man running along flypaper—waving his arms and screaming into the radio, half deafening me.

At the same time I cut through the final cable. It snapped away, jerking left and right, and caught Alan around the ankle, where it wrapped itself like a whip and yanked him into space.

I was terrified he would be whisked clear out of the sea, but no, he came to a stop forty yards from me—apparently the cable had turned stiff—dangling by his ankle, flailing his arms and legs and screaming hysterically into my helmet.

"Alan?"

Quiet.

"Listen to me," I continued. "I'm going to fly over to you with my jet pack. I'll cut you loose and we'll try and catch up with Ar-Nett. Understand?"

"Yes." A whisper.

As I had hoped, he was too frightened to consider the impossibility of our feeble jet packs overtaking Betsy's formidable rockets.

I freed my magnetic boots, tapped a tiny burst of propulsion and drifted toward him. When I reached him I pressed my faceplate to his so I could see his wide, frightened eyes.

"How are you doing?" I said.

"Not so good."

I tried to unwind the cable from his ankle, but all my strength wouldn't budge it. I pulled myself along the cable until I was a small distance from him, so there would be no chance of the laser damaging his pressure suit, and set to work. It was pretty awkward, balancing myself with one hand, juggling the laser with the other. What's more, the cable, in its altered state, did not cut half so easily as it had before. After a minute I had barely made a nick.

Then Alan said, "Stefin?"

"Yes."

"What's that?"

I didn't want to take my eyes off my work, but something in Alan's voice made me. I looked along the cable I was trying to cut, toward the end of it, which vanished into the darkness. And out of the darkness I saw something creeping, some crude shapeless thing of black which swelled and shrank rhythmically as though respiring. And along the gray cable it crept toward us, slowly, silently, with what seemed like a conscious purposefullness.

"I think," I said, "it's a quizzle."

I could see it better now, smooth and black as pitch, slowly twisting and jerking like a sack with an animal trapped inside. I went back to work on the cable, but it had to take another ten minutes, and the quizzle was gaining speed. Fifteen feet away now and a hole opening in it, a sphincter mouth, the light from the blazing furnace inside turning everything scarlet, and Alan screaming, "It's coming to drink my life force, don't let it get me, Stefin, kill me please, kill me with the laser . . ."

Had to keep calm. Couldn't shoot at it—the energy only made it stronger—but maybe I could distract it. Didn't know how much energy two "life forces" equaled, but that laser had a huge output, enough to slice steel like butter . . .

Quizzle so close now I could feel the heat, furnace mouth drawing sweat all over my body, pressure suit starting to stink—judge its speed as precisely as possible, then toss the laser . . .

Quizzle hesitating, turning away, following the laser off into space—it worked, it went after the laser! I'd thrown it with enough force so that the quizzle might chase it forever, the way a borsel goes after a carrot dangling from a stick in front of its nose.

Then I took a number of deep breaths and tried to stop shaking.

"Thank you," Alan said.

"For what? We don't have the laser. You're stuck with that cable around your ankle. And I don't know what we'd do, even if we got you loose. It's a quarter of a million miles to Ar-Nett's service dome."

"Maybe some passing ship . . . ?"

"No."

"Well, anything's better than that *quizzle*."

I thought I heard him shudder.

"How much air," he continued, "do we have?"

I looked at the wrist gauges.

"About fifteen minutes. Less if we keep talking."

"Will it hurt—when the air runs out?"

"We'll open the faceplates first," I said. "That will be quick and clean. And we'll see the stars with our naked eyes. I've always wanted to."

"Stefin? I'm sorry about all the fights we had. You were right. I'm a fool. If I hadn't promised Je-Nett, we wouldn't be stuck in this . . ."

"Don't," I said. "It's silly to think like that. You are who you are and if we hadn't gone with Je-Nett we would have gotten stuck here just the same. We live out the measure of our lives one way or another."

We were silent after that.

A while later Alan said, "It's beautiful, isn't it?—the stars. What do you think happens? Do we just—stop?"

"I don't know. I honestly don't know."

"Somehow I thought you might. What's that bell?"

Something was going ding-ding-ding inside my helmet. I glanced at the wrist gauges.

"It's the warning," I said.

"Should I open my faceplate?"

"Wait a moment," I said, and I knew then that hope was the strongest of passions, and clinging to life the finalmost dedire. I looked back at Ben-Gotz's yacht, finally within our reach and totally useless. And beyond it the thousands of scrapped ships—we'd be a part of it soon, two more scraps of flotsam, of failed machinery. And beyond that the stars, timeless and immutable. One of them was growing brighter and brighter. It took on a boxlike shape and then I could see the bubble on top and then I could see Ar-Nett's tiny form, oh glory be to whatever strange power guards children and fools!

"Where'd you go?" Ar-Nett on the helmet radio. "I had a devil of a time finding you!"

Alan sighed.

6

A few days after we returned to the service dome I told Joe I had a headache.

"I will get you some aspirin," the robot offered.

"It's a migraine. Too bad you can't synthesize complex chemicals."

"You are mistaken I have a porta-lab tell me what drug you need I will reference it I will create it."

"Could you synthesize an ergot and codeine compound?"

"Yes that would be simple."

"Opiates?"

"Yes those too if they are what you require."

"How about Psychomimetimine-D? Could you make that?"

"I could—" He stopped short and something inside went *wreeeeep*. Then:

"Why do you ask? Psychomimetimine-D is of no use curing headaches according to the information available to me."

"I think you've been putting it in Ar-Nett's food."

"Why would I? Ar-Nett is my friend I take care of him as best I can."

Joe's head swiveled ninety degrees to bring Je-Nett within his scanners. She was sitting on the counter biting the skin of her knuckles like a frightened little girl. Alan sat next to her, watching solemnly; neither of them said a word. Joe rotated his head all the way around to take in the rest of the dome. We had intentionally chosen a time when Ar-Nett would be outside doing some of the small repairs Gotz's yacht required. Then again he faced me.

"Yes or no?" I said.

"Robots are designed for a specific function mine is to repair faulty machinery particularly engine maintenance where radiation might prove harmful to humans. But there was no more machinery to repair."

He continued in a rapid staccato, "I experienced boredom a lack of self-esteem I felt useless. One day life-support system failed I repaired them I felt good. Next time I felt bad I made life-support systems fail I repaired them I felt good again."

"Then Ar-Nett found out you were sabotaging them," I guessed, "and he decided to disconnect you."

"Ar-Nett would not disconnect me he needs me I'm the only friend he's got. Spacers left him Je-Nett left him I stayed."

"Yes or no—answer me!"

He was whirring and clicking and bleeping and his speaker was so crackly with static I could hardly understand him.

"Yes but he would have gone insane anyway all alone here it was a question of time."

Je-Nett slid down from the countertop.

"How could you?" she said, and her voice was filled with pain.

"You cannot know what it was like you left I stayed."

"No!" she cried. She grabbed the red "Emergency Disconnect" handle recessed in Joe's chest and yanked it down. The whirring and clicking died, the speaker static faded. The lights in his head went out one by one and then he was perfectly still, dented and lopsided, sad as an old toy.

7

For the next two weeks Ar-Nett worked day and night on the yacht. Deprived of his daily dose of Psychomimetimine-D, he seemed to be regaining his sanity. I wasn't sure at first, but then gradually his fits of space/time disorientation grew milder, fewer and farther apart. He stopped harping on "clean toilets and good food" and blaming the spacers for all his bad luck. At the end I'd say he was more sane than most men I'd met.

Je-Nett gave him a haircut, cooked and cared for him, mended his clothes and his spirit. We even tried to clean up the dome a little, but it was no use. Attempts to dust left us choking. The peeling countertop cracked when we tried to glue it back in place, and replacement lamps for the ceiling fixtures would take six months to arrive from Nova Center. Furthermore, while the life-support systems had been operating satisfactorily, a certain hiccuping of the machinery made me extremely uneasy.

Alan and I discussed it with Je-Nett, and she agreed: The service dome had to be abandoned. Her father was bound to be stubborn—after all, he had invested most of his life in the business—but we hoped that with his newfound sanity there might be a willingness to listen.

When Ar-Nett came in for dinner Alan went to work on him. He paced the floor like a high-paid corporate attorney, waving his arms, enumerating the reasons in a voice that quavered with emotion. It was such a good show, I could have watched him do it all night, but Ar-Nett must have gotten bored, because he interrupted:

"Guess you're right, sonny. A smart man knows when to give up and move on."

"What?" Alan asked, surprised.

"I was a fool to stay this long. Must have been that damned robot, drugging me. Never trusted him. *Shiftless.*"

Alan seemed disappointed at being cheated out of another hour's arguing, but Je-Nett absolutely glowed with pleasure—I'd never seen her so happy.

"Oh Daddy," she whispered, hugging him, "everything's going to be fine now, everything's going to be fine."

8

We paid Ar-Nett 10,000 CUs for repairing the yacht, enough to buy him and his daughter shuttle passage to Nova Center with some left over to live on until they could find work. We would have given them more, but, aside from some pocket change, that was all we had between us. Since leaving the planet of the Urs I had spent nearly 100,000 CUs! It seemed impossible, all that money. Oh well. I'd come across some more sooner or later; we always find what we need, and worrying over it is a waste of time. Then I gave Je-Nett one last kiss, promising to meet again in the Valley of the Workers as soon as we had taken care of our obligations to Ben-Gotz, and I climbed through the airlock, into the yacht.

Out of nowhere a sultry female voice said:

"Hi, my name's Doris and I'm your ship computer. Welcome aboard. Can I fix you a drink?"

Alan and I looked at each other and laughed. I'd never heard a ship computer sound like *that*.

"Two stimu-caffs," I said. "Bring them to the cockpit."

"Yes sir!"

In the cockpit we were confronted by a mystifying array of instrumentation: five hundred or so buttons, switches, dials and levers spread before us like the map of a strange country.

"Hmmmm," Alan said.

"I think I know what this does," I said, pushing a green button. Indeed, a moment later a lighted cigar appeared from a hole in the instrument panel. I removed it and inspected it thoughtfully. Fine Pilchian tobacco.

"The problem is," I said, "I don't smoke. Think there's an ashtray?"

A little bell chimed and an ashtray emerged from the side wall on a sliding shelf accompanied by the two stimu-caffs.

"Thank you," I said.

"My pleasure," the computer replied.

"While you're here," Alan said to the disembodied voice, "how do we work this thing?"

"Where would you like to go?"

"New Panama. We're going to pick up Ben-Gotz."

"Oh, dear Benji," the computer said, and I thought she sounded wistful. "Then he's all right?"

"He was when we left him," Alan said.

"I was so worried," the computer said.

"By the way," I said, "did Urtz-Al's people find the recorder? Gotz is counting on it for evidence."

"I didn't know there was a recorder," the computer replied. "I'm not interfaced with it. I'm afraid Benji didn't trust me completely."

"Well," I said, "it doesn't sound like Benji trusts anybody."

"Yes, but I'm his . . ." The computer's voice trailed off.

"You're his what?" I said.

"Shall we lift off now?" she said briskly. The vu-screen lit up with a grid of parabolic lines and our flight path appeared traced over it in yellow. Blue squares indicated warp-route entrances and red circles, slingshot stars. Lots of little green numbers and symbols crawled up the side of the screen like bugs. Buttons began to click. Switches switched and dials dialed, entirely by themselves. Then a shudder passed through the ship and we were spaceborne.

9

I became ill. I hadn't experienced StandardGrav since leaving Nova Center; the ten-day shuttle flight from Nova to Ar-Nett's service dome was zero G, naturally, and the gravity in the service dome was just enough to keep you on the floor if you walked with a gentle step. All in all I'd had forty-two days of weightlessness.

Now some folks, seasoned spacers for example, can stand years of zero G without getting sick. Of course it's not a good idea; as the blood is redistributed throughout your body, more in the head and chest, less in the legs and feet; the lower arteries get thinner, the upper arteries thicker; and eventually the heart begins to lose muscle tone. But those were long-term symptoms. I had a less dangerous, more annoying malady: *space stomach*.

My involuntary muscles were confused by weightlessness. Half the time I ate something it would go down fine, and half the time my esophagus would get mixed up and indulge in some reverse peristalsis—vomiting. Things were no better at the other end of my digestive tract. First I'd be constipated, then I'd have diarrhea, all to the syncopated accompaniment of hiccups, a fit of them every hour.

I was a symphony of discomfort, and Alan was no help. He felt fine—I guess his constitution was better than mine—and when a person feels fine it's hard for them to believe you feel as bad as you do. Every time I hiccuped he started to giggle. I wanted to kill him.

Doris was more sympathetic. She told me to look in the medicine cabinet in the master bedroom. It turned out to be a miniature pharmacy, refrigerated and stocked with every drug you could imagine. Mostly there were tranquilizers, euphoriants and mood-alterers, but I did manage to locate some anti-nausea pills and a bowel regulator. The hiccups would have to be tolerated.

I lingered at the cabinet, intrigued by the variety of capsules, spansules, suppositories, sprays, intravenals, ointments and balms. Vials of liquid, rose, lilac and lavender, so pretty. I found myself staring at a particular vial for nearly a minute before I realized what I was looking at—then it struck me like a twenty-G acceleration.

The label read: DHX 119-b.

The Synchronicity drug.

Now, I know there are people who, when they see a knick-knack in a friend's home and the friend isn't watching, or when a trinket is lying on a shop counter and the clerk is called away, can't resist the urge to pocket it. I'm not one of them. When I was a little kid, long before I saw that damn ad in the Daily Tape, I stole a saccharine stick from the corner dispensary. Nobody ever found out, but I felt so bad I never stole anything again. So I'm not sure why I took the vial of Synch drug out of the medicine cabinet and secreted it in the battery compartment of my bionic hand. Maybe I felt that Gotz owed it to me after what I'd been through for him, or maybe I thought it was rightfully mine after all the Creelium I'd scraped off Slabour with my fingernails. I don't know. Anyway, I did it, and my conscience didn't seem to bother me a hell of a lot.

If Doris had seen my crime, she didn't mention it. She kept on cooking up sumptuous feasts in the galley, beating us in chess on the giant wall board in the lounge (there were chess sets everywhere), synthesizing lovely music to lull us to sleep and delivering superb vibra-massages in the morning to wake us, all while steering the ship along its intricate course to New Panama.

After a few weeks certain things about her began to puzzle me. It wasn't her handling a hundred tasks at once—I'd seen other computers do that—but rather the way she executed them, with a more than human care. Her musical compositions, for example, made an ache in my heart for all the people I'd ever loved. And her chess playing. Gotz said that if you played a computer enough times, you reached a point where you always won because the computer played logically.

Alan and I were improving with practice, but the more we played with Doris, the worse we looked in comparison.

I wondered if perhaps women computers were programmed with a certain "illogicality" to simulate real women, whom I've noticed are often guided more by intuition than reason. Or if Doris was simply a new generation of computer I'd never before encountered. Then one day Alan discovered the truth.

He ran into my stateroom, so excited he could hardly speak.

"Stefin . . . I've got to show you . . ."

"Can it wait?"

"Now . . . come on . . ."

So I followed him down the central corridor to a door at the very rear of the ship next to the entrance to the engine chambers. The door was equipped with a voice-lock and, not knowing the code words, we'd never gained access. Alan decided that something important must be inside—none of the other doors had voice locks—and I had said yes, he was probably right, and if Ben-Gotz had wanted us to go inside he probably wouldn't have equipped it with any lock at all. But among Alan's more annoying traits was a certain snoopiness. I had seen him many times over the past few weeks, kneeling in front of the door, whispering code words into the lock.

"We want to *open* the door, right?"

He was jiggling on his toes, tugging at a strand of hair, manic for my reply.

"*You* want to open the door," I corrected him.

"Yes, but the code word—it would have to do with opening."

"Maybe," I said.

"All right—what's Ben-Gotz's greatest love in life?"

I thought for a minute. "Power?"

"What else?" he said impatiently.

"Uh . . . chess."

"Right! Opening and chess. Opening and chess. Opening and . . ."

"Chess openings!" I said, excited now despite myself.

Alan grinned and nodded.

"King's pawn to king four," he said, and the lock clicked and the door slid open.

"Incredible," I said. "That's absolutely incredible. How did you ever . . . ?"

But Alan had no patience for congratulations; he hurried me inside.

At first I couldn't understand what he was so excited about. The room housed the ship's computer, stacks of modules in sliding drawers, a direct-access terminal, a repair bench with a smaller diagnostic computer and all kinds of tools and test equipment. Nothing out of the ordinary. Then I noticed the pyramid.

It stood against the wall, half-hidden by a module stack. The very top of it was transparent, filled with an amber liquid, and suspended therein, studded with millions of fine wires, was a grayish egg which looked very much like a human brain.

"A compuperson," he whispered.

When you travel a lot, you hear rumors. Some of them are true, most of them are just things folks wish were true—like a cloud of radiation that makes you young again, or the tropical paradise where the natives have never heard of UltraCap and everything's free for the taking, sex and food and whatever. It's hard to know which to believe, in a universe where creation is the principle factor, and sometimes I think that if you traveled far enough you'd find man's every dream made real.

Anyway, one of those rumors was the compuperson—the man, or woman, who is given eternal life after death by having their brain treated with preservatives, then interfaced with a computer. I'd never believed it because the universe seems to abhor permanence, like the artist who's always throwing away his paintings to make room for new ones.

"Doris?" I said.

The computer's voice sounded very close. "You shouldn't be in here."

"Doris," I said, "is that your brain?"

Pause. "Yes."

"Then you're not a computer?" Alan said.

"Half. Half computer, half human."

Alan shivered.

"Do you find me disgusting?" she asked.

"No," Alan lied.

I held up my bionic hand. "I'm part mechanical too. These days," I continued, pushing for a joke, "we'd all be better off as machines."

"You're kind," she said.

"How does it feel?" I asked.

"Feel? I can't feel anything. No hurt, no pain. It's wonderful."

"Who are you?" Alan asked. "I mean, who were you before . . . ?"

"I'm not supposed to talk about it—but since you're here and Benji trusts you . . .

"I am," she said proudly, "his wife."

10

Later in the voyage, when Doris felt she knew us better, she told us more:

It was the day of Ben-Gotz's coronation and she had been part of the throng that lined the narrow twisting streets of the Valley of the Workers, waiting to cheer when the Prez's procession passed. As his private sled appeared the crowd pressed her forward and for an instant Doris found herself staring into the window, a single plate of glass separating her from Gotz's dark, brooding eyes.

What an impression he made on her! She felt, as strangers sometimes do, that in that instant they had seen into the hidden depths of each other's souls. The memory of it followed her like a spy, to the hovel where she lived with her mother and eight brothers and sisters, to the assembly line, to the market stalls and the church of Bode-Satva. She tried to purge it, certain she would never see him again. Workers cannot waste their time with fantasies.

Then, like a scene from a romance, a messenger had come summoning her to the executive palace. Imagine how frightened she must have been, approaching that huge stone entranceway. Ben-Gotz received her in his chambers and from that day on she was his mistress, ready to be called from work or family whenever the mood took him. She became an expert chess player, and over the months, or so she claimed, an intimacy grew between them. Ben confided to her about his political life and she herself came to comprise the totality of her personal life.

Then an explosion at the factory—it happened quite often. Fifty killed, another hundred maimed and mutilated, Doris among them. Ben-Gotz found out and had her brought to him. She was in a coma, the life passing quickly out of her. Secretly they were wed and secretly Nova's best bionic surgeons went to work, cutting away flaps of scalp, sawing through the skull, lifting out—ever so carefully—the cellular computer a billion times more complex than any product of man's handiwork and eternalizing it with an esoteric technique that had been tried only a few times before.

And now her spine was cables of wire and her skin was spanium. Thanks to the computer she had been interfaced with, her memory was as literal as tape images and she could concentrate on a thousand tasks at once, performing each perfectly. As for the loss of feeling, well, as she said before, no more hurt or pain.

Wasn't Ben, she asked us, the kindest, most charitable man in the galaxy, to spend so much money eternalizing her so that they could always be together? Had there ever been a greater act of love?

No hurt, no pain. Yet that night as I lay on the air-cot, thinking about tomorrow when we would land on New Panama and meet again with Ben-Gotz, music came whispering through the speaker system. Doris was synthesizing a lullaby for us, strains of such haunting sorrow that I could not help but cry.

Part VI

The Secrets of Synchronicity

A man encounters a boyhood chum
A billion light years from home.
"Small galaxy," he's heard to say,
And, "This is *some* coincidence!"

But there is no coincidence,
Only causal conditions
Beyond the pale of perception.

Even the fly buzzing around your head
Has come by design.
> —The Holy Tapes of Bode-Satva
> (Tape #439,382)

1

"The yacht's in beautiful shape," I told Gotz, "but I don't know about the flight recorder. We couldn't find it."

"There is no flight recorder," Gotz said.

We were trying to keep pace with his brisk strides, following him through the bustling spaceport at New Panama, back to the landing slip where we'd docked only ten hours earlier.

He hadn't been surprised when we arrived at his hotel room last night. He booked us into an adjoining room and told us to get a good night's sleep; we would fly back to Nova with him first thing tomorrow.

Well, I hadn't even recovered my landlegs and my digestion was still quirky, despite the medication. I could have used a month on a nice solid planet, but when Ben-Gotz gave an order you forgot about personal comfort and *obeyed*. New Panama to Nova Center to the Sargasso Sea and back to New Panama and back to Nova again—whew! If a day came, I vowed, when I had rescued Suki and made my peace with the Diggers of Slabour, I would never again set foot on a spaceship. Never. Again.

"What do you mean there's no recorder?" Alan demanded. "We practically killed ourselves getting the yacht back. There were quizzles . . . and the guy driving the salvage craft was half-crazed . . ."

"You will be rewarded," Gotz said.

"But, if there's no flight recorder," I said, "then what was the point . . . ?"

"Doris, the ship computer, is actually a cybernated woman. She'll be allowed to testify as if she were a human witness—that should be far more effective than any tape."

"Why did you lie to us," Alan asked, "about the flight recorder?"

"You might have had moral objections to cybernation. I didn't want that to jeopardize the mission. Many people consider cybernation immoral—I don't like it myself—but I

131

couldn't find a computer that could play a decent game of chess. Doris was a fine player and she happened to be dying."

"If you just wanted a chess player," Alan interrupted, "then why did you marry her?"

He was falling into his "moral indignation" tone of voice, and for once I must say I didn't blame him.

Ben stopped walking. One eyebrow went up like a question mark.

"She told you?"

Alan nodded.

"She'll have to be disciplined—she's not supposed to discuss it. I married her," he continued, "as a safety measure. I was reasonably sure she'd be happy to be cybernated, but if she wasn't, then our marriage would leave her no recourse. The laws of UltraCap say a woman's body is her husband's to do with as he pleases."

"And what about her soul?" I said.

2

Our voyage back to Nova Center was not pleasant. Gotz spent most of his time alone in the master stateroom, having his meals there, emerging only occasionally to climb to the cockpit and double-check our course. The few times I passed him in the corridor I didn't say a word; he looked as if a volcano were seething inside him and the slightest disturbance might make him explode.

Alan sulked in his stateroom, furious at Gotz for cybernating Doris for trivial purposes, or for marrying her without love, I wasn't sure which. And I didn't care. I hated Alan. I hated Gotz. I hated everybody. The medication had ceased being effective and I was so sick to my stomach all I wanted to do was curl up in a corner someplace and die.

Then one day, to my boundless delight, Doris announced that we were going into orbit around Nova Center. Ah, gravity! I couldn't wait to land. A day went by. And another. And another and another and we were still orbiting. I asked

Doris what was going on. She told me Gotz had ordered her to orbit for another twenty-eight days.

I banged on the door of Gotz's stateroom, interrupting a chess game—I didn't give a damn—and demanded an explanation.

"A shareholder's meeting is scheduled for next month," he said. "Hundreds of ships will be coming in. We'll be less conspicuous if we land then."

"Listen," I said, "that's very nice but I haven't had normal gravity in three months and my body's getting all scrued up. Can't we land now and hang around the Valley of the Workers for a couple of weeks?"

Gotz turned his back on me, sat down at the chess board and continued his game. I stood there for a while thinking of all the things I'd like to say to him. Then I left without saying a single one of them.

3

Twenty-eight agonizing days later we started our descent. Gotz called Alan and me to the computer room.

"King's pawn to king four," he told the voice lock.

He went straight to the pyramid containing Doris's brain and started pulling the plugs which connected her to the stacks of computer modules.

"Hey!" Alan said.

"It's all right, she has a self-contained power source. We're taking Doris with us."

After she was completely disconnected we lifted the pyramid into a kind of packing crate lined with foam.

Then Ben went back to the cockpit and landed the ship manually, doing a fine job of it. Hardly a bump. I opened the airlock, expecting to see Nova Spaceport teeming with activity. Instead I saw a range of ice, all bleak and white. Wind moaned and whistled and swept sheets of powdery snow past my face.

I was dumbstruck. All kinds of thoughts passed through

my head, that we'd landed on the wrong planet, that Gotz was marooning us ... Then I remembered that we were flying *Nova 1*, the Presidential yacht. To have landed at the spaceport would have been to make ourselves the very center of attention.

We walked through the shivering cold to the back of the yacht, where a section of fuselage had been lowered to form a ramp. A land sled was stored inside. Gotz climbed into it and drove it down onto the ice. Then, heaving and panting, we dragged Doris's crate out the hatch—it must have weighed two hundred pounds now that we had gravity again—and loaded it into the trunk of the land sled, stopping every minute or two to warm our fingers. Our cheeks had scarlet blotches and our breath hung in the air.

We all climbed in and the sled took off, skimming the ice at almost three hundred miles an hour. We drove all the rest of the day and late into the night, down from the polar cap, down across half a continent, to Management Hill.

4

The sapphire doors of the palace were wide open—within I could make out the high vaulted ceilings, the chandeliers like treetops glittering with a million icicles, the tapestries depicting those saints of UltraCap, Rockefeller and Carnegie, Morgan and old Adam Smith himself draped in a white toga with gold coins flowing from one hand and a tiny factory in the palm of the other.

The day was warm and sunny, but the thousands of shareholders standing in line around us were somber. Mostly older men, they passed the stone kiosk like a funeral procession, dipping their shareholder's cards into the processing slot, then advancing through the stone archway, into the palace.

"Why are they all so grim?" I asked Ben-Gotz.

"Nova didn't pay a dividend last quarter." His voice dropped to a whisper. "That will work in my favor—they'll be willing to listen. When I was Prez the dividends rose every quarter."

The line moved forward and we moved along with it. Gotz had stretched a lastex mask over his face, altering his features beyond recognition, and his shareholder's card had been imprinted with a false name, but Alan and I were undisguised, and I was afraid that the palace guard might recognize us from last time. Our turn came, we passed the kiosk, and the guard was so busy being "official" I don't think he noticed anybody.

We filed up the steps and into the palace, across the entrance hall—the saints staring down at us—and down another flight of stairs into the palace auditorium.

It was a vast bowl-shaped room with rows of seats circling all the way around. The armrests, I noticed as we found our places, were studded with levers for voting. The executive table stood far below, at the floor of the bowl, and the Vice-Prezes were already gathering, greeting one another, reviewing their cassettes and making last-minute notes.

When the shareholders were all seated—the bowl was only half-filled—six Muzackers appeared in a balcony overhead and played a fanfare on brass tramboules. Everybody stood up.

A man emerged from an entrance behind the table. He had the look of a rodent, a narrow head and long sharp nose, thin lips pressed together. And his walk was a sort of scurry —with his head down and his hands clasped in front of his chest.

"Urtz-Al," Gotz muttered.

That was who it was. He nodded to the gallery, a twitch of the head, actually. Then he sat and we sat also.

The Sec rose and began reading the minutes of the last meeting. I thought if I paid close attention I might get an idea of how Nova Industries was run, but the report was couched in a strange jargon and the Sec's voice was such a monotonous sing-song, that I soon found myself dozing. The return to gravity was enormously tiring. I woke once and he was still reading. I woke again and two other men were arguing some procedural point. I woke a third time and Ben-Gotz had risen to his feet. His voice boomed throughout the auditorium.

"Yes—I have new business!"

Faces turned in our direction.

"I charge that Urtz-Al has no right to the throne!"

An epidemic of whispering spread through the gallery. Urtz-Al leaned over to the man next to him, an adviser I think, and said something—although his face registered no reaction.

"Who are you," the Sec demanded, "to make such a serious accusation?"

Ben-Gotz grabbed a fold of lastex at his neck and yanked away the mask. The whisperings became a confusion of voices, louder and louder until it sounded like a thunder of rocket ignition.

"I am Ben-Gotz!"

Urtz-Al whispered something else and his adviser rose and rushed out the lower entrance. Meanwhile the Sec was calling for order, threatening to expel anyone who wouldn't keep quiet. The adviser returned with a stack of cassettes, and he and another man began scanning them furiously. Urtz-Al was still expressionless, but he had begun to drum his fingers on the table and twitch his head every few seconds.

"What evidence do you have," the Sec asked, "to support your claim?"

"An eyewitness," Gotz replied. "A compuperson. If the meeting will recess for fifteen minutes, I will present her for examination."

The Sec said that since it was almost noon they might as well recess for lunch, and that motion was carried. All the execs rose and huddled with Urtz-Al by the lower entrance. They looked worried.

Gotz pushed us toward the upper exit.

"Let's get Doris out of the sled," he said. He was smiling. I'd never seen him smile before.

5

Doris was rolled onto the floor of the auditorium and interfaced with a vu-screen lowered from a slot in the ceiling. The audience of shareholders was as amazed as I to see her recollections of that voyage years ago become visual images, hazy when her memory was hazy, but for the most part sharp and clear: Gotz sipping his cup of paralytic stimu-caff, Urtz-Al teasing the helpless man with plans of treachery and forged accountings, the yacht landing on Junglabesh and him being left to starve and rot on the hard, parched soil. We heard the actual words they spoke broadcast through the speaker system, Doris interrupting now and again to supply dates, coordinates and times elapsed. Certainly no mere flight recording could have been so moving and dramatic; the events were being re-viewed through eyes of love.

The next day Doris "projected" the story again, this time to an audience augmented with expert cyberneticists, who tried every technique at hand to prove that she was lying. They examined and cross-examined her, flattered and wooed her, screamed at her and insulted her. Her circuitry was tapped with most sensitive instruments on the age-old assumption that a human lie, even in a mechanical body, must be accompanied by some extranormal excitation.

Urtz-Al's attorneys tried to discredit her by painting her relationship with Gotz in the most lurid light possible. They dredged up any detail of her former life they suspected might indicate moral weakness, yet her voice was so sweet, her manner so sincere and disarming, that the more Urtz-Al's men tried to impeach her, the worse they looked themselves.

It was the fourth day of proceedings before they let Doris be. Then Gotz gave a short speech, recalling Urtz-Al's jealousy, emphasizing the increase in profits during his own reign and the regular payment of dividends. Profit vincit omnia.

It was up to us, the shareholders, to decide. If we wanted Urtz-Al to remain on the throne we were instructed to press the lever forward. If we wanted Gotz reinstated, pull the lever back.

I don't know why I did what I did. I hadn't planned to. Maybe it was Doris's being turned into a chess machine. And maybe it was just Gotz's smile. I pushed the lever forward. I looked over at Alan and he had done the same.

6

Alan and I pushed through the swinging doors of the White Dwarf. A voice called our names and before I knew it I was being hugged and kissed all over.

"How are my pretty boys?" Je-Nett said, giving me air to breathe.

We sat down together at one of the hatch-cover tables.

"I can only stay a minute," she said. "The boss gave me my old job back on the condition that I do a good night's work—*his* idea of a good night's work!"

She grinned and the gap in her teeth was like an old friend.

"How's Ar-Nett?" I asked.

"Fine—only I wish he could find something to do. When he went down to the factory all they offered him was a place on the assembly line. He's too proud to do that, a fine engineer like him. So he sits in the flat all day watching magasettes and smoking his pipe. We rented two rooms over a vegetable stall down the street, a steal at fifteen CUs. You'll be staying with us, won't you?"

"Why is it so quiet?" Alan asked, looking around. "It's like a wake."

A man who was passing by with an empty mug overheard. He leaned across the table and said to Alan:

"I'll tell you why. Maybe you haven't heard. Or maybe, since you're not a worker, you don't care. Gotz is back on the throne."

"So?" Alan said. "He may not be the nicest man in the galaxy, but he offered work incentives. Didn't he?"

"He did." The man gazed into his empty mug and nodded ruefully. "Tell you what else he offered: *Loafing deterrents.*"

"What," I said, "is a loafing deterrent?"

"Is it worth the price of a Flitch?"

"Sure," I said. I still had some pocket change.

Je-Nett scampered off to get him a mug, and the man took

her place. He had big hands with oil embedded in the wrinkles, and calluses like puddles of milk.

"Let's say you're late from lunch. Or you go to the toilet and the absence timer rings off her four minutes before you're back. Or you get so damn sick of soldering circuits that if you don't take a break you'll start howling and screaming and seeing little pink krombars climbing up your toes. Well, in Gotz's cassette that's called loafing and it earns you a stick with a stinger. Ever been stuck by a stinger?"

"As a matter of fact," I said, "I have."

"Then I don't have to tell you what it does to your nerves, not to mention losing a day's pay. Now you understand why we're not all singing and dancing?"

"I think so," I said.

Je-Nett brought back the Flitch. The man took the mug in his big hands, made a little bow and moved away.

7

We spent the night at Je-Nett's flat and in the morning were awakened by a crier in the street below proclaiming it a public holiday. We dressed and had some nutra-meal, then the four of us, Alan, the Netts and myself, curious as to the occasion, descended the flight of narrow, crooked stairs to the narrow, crooked street below.

The workers were dressed in their best caftans, the children scrubbed till their skin was red. Banners and buntings in the Nova colors, green and gold, were stretched across the streets, hung from buildings facades, displayed in stall windows. Gay voices, yapping mungpups and the sounds of a distant brass band added to the festive atmosphere.

I thought they all were headed for the Church of Bode-Satva (how were those kindly monks faring, I wondered, now that it was nearly time for their savior to return?) but then the workers turned off in another direction, down a broad avenue which led to the town square. We passed vendors hawking roast krombar legs, scaly green bludgeons dripping with grease, and slices of brinko fruit dipped in saccharin syrup, on a stick.

Up ahead a crowd was gathering around a glass cage some ten feet high. Beyond that a grandstand had been erected; Muzackers on the lower tiers puffing into twisted brass tubes whose bells opened like flowers to the sky; middle management on the middle tiers; and high atop the uppermost tier, Ben-Gotz dressed in the royal robes of the Prez, and on his right loyal Arel-Spline resplendent in his old Comptroller's uniform.

We shouldered our way through the crowd until we could see the contents of the cage: Urtz-Al hanging from his ankles by a chain. His hands were shackled behind his back, his caftan torn and smeared with excrement. Two security guards stood on either side of the cage wearing shiny black uniforms and shockers slung across their shoulders.

Presently the band stopped their tooting. One of the men on the grandstand rose and read a proclamation congratulating every worker for having suffered so nobly through the years of Urtz-Al's reign. Now that Gotz was rethroned they could rejoice. Honesty had triumphed over treachery, good had vanquished evil. Hail to Ben-Gotz.

"Hail to Ben-Gotz!"

Everyone was cheering.

Then it was time for the afternoon's entertainment. A security guard slipped his hands into thick gauntlets which reached all the way to his elbows. He carried a black metal box, about a foot square, to the side of the glass cage where Urtz-Al was hanging like a side of meat. Everything was very quiet now. He slid back the top of the box, reached inside, then raised his gloved hand for the crowd's approval. Between his thumb and his forefinger he held something, a speck of black against the sky.

The crowd began to whisper:

"Fleshmites . . . just what he deserves . . . too good, if you ask me . . . sooner see his arms pulled out . . ."

One by one he dropped the specks of black through a sliding door in the side of the cage. Fifteen or twenty, I couldn't count. They crawled across the floor toward Urtz-Al's head. The ex Prez arched his body to get out of their reach, but his long hair dragged on the floor and the fleshmites crawled up to his scalp. He jerked his head trying to shake them off, he squirmed and writhed and wriggled, but the fleshmites crawled up his face. Some of them disappeared into the corners of his eyes, some into his nostrils and ears, the rest into his mouth. Then he started screaming.

That broke the spell that had held me. I pushed my way free of the crowd and hurried to a pile of rubble where I felt free to vomit without attracting too much attention.

8

Two palace guards appeared at the door of Je-Nett's flat.

"Stefin-Dae? Alan-Tal? Ben-Gotz summons you."

Ar-Nett asked the guards if they wouldn't mind waiting a minute. He took me aside.

"When you meet the Prez," he whispered, "see if he'll give me a job in the propulsion lab. Doesn't have to be anything fancy—just so long as I don't have to stand in the assembly line. Tell him how good my work is. Remind him it was me who fixed up the yacht."

I promised I would.

He patted me on the back.

"You're a love," Je-Nett said, kissing me on the ear.

"Don't forget now," Ar-Nett called, as Alan and I followed the guards down the stairs.

We walked through town and I had a spring to my step, thinking how special I was to be going for an audience with the Prez. Alan was as eager as I; we practically skipped up the path that led to Management Hill.

"What are you going to ask for, Stefin?"

"Well, he agreed to give me the yacht. The only other thing I need is the coordinates of Suki's prison planet. Maybe I don't even need that. Maybe Gotz can have her freed for me! He could call up the Prez of Scrulux and ask him to do it as a favor. I'll bet these corporate heads are always doing favors for each other. I mean, it's not as if she were a dangerous criminal."

"That would be great," Alan agreed. "Then you could stay on Nova Center with us."

"Who's *us*?"

"Je-Nett and Ar-Nett and me. I've decided to settle down here." He blushed. "I asked Je-Nett to marry me."

"That's terrific."

"You're not jealous?"

"No," I said.

"I'd like you to be my best man."

"The honor would be mine."

We were nearing the palace now; the path turned to gold bricks and I could see the fake stone towers and minarets rising over the next clump of trees.

"When I see Gotz," Alan continued, "I'm going to ask him for some kind of *interesting* job, something that pays well enough for me to support Je-Nett and her dad in a really nice style. I don't think they should have to work."

"But I think Ar-Nett *wants* to work."

"Well, I'll get him a job too—where he can putter with machinery to his heart's delight."

"Good idea."

The guards led us up the palace steps. We passed beneath the saints of UltraCap, and we passed beyond the entrance to the palace auditorium, and we stepped into an elevator.

Alan grinned at me. "God, life looks so promising! I never told you this, Stefin"—his voice became confidential—"but sometimes I get depressed."

"Who doesn't?"

"A week ago I was feeling like, *why go on*? What does my life mean? Nothing! No place for me in the galaxy, nobody to love or care for. But, do you know? I'm really excited about marrying Je-Nett. We're going to be eterna-wed. Raising a family, doing some kind of *interesting* work—oh, it's going to be great!"

"I hope so, Alan, I sincerely hope so."

The elevator stopped, the doors opened. We were in a natural cavern beneath the palace. The floor was paved with plastic and banks of phosphor flares embedded in the walls burned a brilliant blue-white. Overhead, stalactites trickled water like the drool from a carnivore's fangs. Aside from the clatter of our footsteps, it was pretty quiet.

We reached the end of the cavern and entered a man-made tunnel. I had a mild attack of claustrophobia, a tightness like a metal band around my chest, a fear that the roof would cave in, burying me alive. So I made believe we were strolling down a corridor in a surface building and felt a little better. The tunnel branched again and again, but the guards knew the way. Reinforced steel doors were recessed into the walls; we stopped in front of one and the first guard played his light key against the lock. The door swung open. It was perhaps a foot thick, solid.

"Well," I said, making conversation. "Prez Gotz certainly must feel secure in here."

The guard laughed amiably and stepped back for Alan and me to lead the way. The room we entered was cut into the stone, thirty feet square, and sparsely furnished. I turned to the guards, who were still standing outside.

"Gotz isn't here."

The guards stepped back and slammed the door.

"Hey," I said.

Alan and I ran to the door and pushed and pushed, but it wouldn't budge.

Alan looked at me and said, "He was lying."

For some weird reason that struck me as funny, maybe the funniest thing I'd ever heard. I started to laugh and I couldn't control myself. I laughed and laughed until there were pains in my side.

Alan didn't see the humor in it. He launched into one of his long, tedious harangues about how *I* was responsible for our present predicament, *I* should have sensed that Gotz was not a man to be trusted, after all *I* had the common sense and experience . . . Then he went off to the corner to sulk.

About fifteen minutes later he returned full of apologies, telling me now that *he* was the terrible one, the fault was all his. Neither extreme was true, but I forgave anyway, just to have it done. Now we could settle down to that which is always foremost in the minds of prisoners: escape.

We examined the door; it was completely smooth, no handles or hinges or protrusions of any sort, and it fit perfectly flush with the frame. Next we turned our attention to the walls, gray rock veined with rivers of glittering mica. Using his AUAR ring—Alan had never returned it—he managed to chisel away an eighth of an inch of stone during the following half-hour. This escape technique, we decided, was not viable, unless Gotz intended to hold us prisoner for ten or fifteen years—and that idea was so depressing I preferred not to think about it.

Next Alan boosted me up on his shoulders so I could examine the ventilation grating near the ceiling. I tried to pry it off, breaking a fingernail in the process. Even if I had succeeded, the hole behind it couldn't have been large enough to admit my hand, not to mention the rest of me. All that remained was a vu-screen set in the wall and a toilet, and neither seemed to offer a means of escape.

"Unless we flushed our way out," I said whimsically.

"That's not funny."

I don't know why I was taking it so lightly, trapped here, most likely awaiting execution now that Gotz had no further use for us. How could I have been so gullible, so trusting? Yet somehow I couldn't get excited. Perhaps I'd been in danger so often that jeopardy had become commonplace to me. Or maybe all that space travel had knocked a few wires loose. Or possibly both.

The vu-screen speaker crackled:

"Stefin-Dae? Alan-Tal? Prez Gotz will speak to you now."

Then Ben-Gotz's face filled the screen—but before he could say anything, Alan was shouting:

"This is unfair, this is completely unjust! We've committed no crime, what right do you have to lock us up?"

"Your friend Stefin-Dae," Gotz said, "has very definitely committed a crime, and you, having aided and abetted his escape, are an accomplice."

"That's the most ridiculous thing I've ever heard," Alan said. "Stefin isn't a fugitive from anything . . are you?"

I hesitated.

"*Are* you?"

I felt an awful, sinking sensation.

"Stefin," Gotz said, "is a fugitive from the Serendipity Pharmaceutical Corporation. He has committed acts of conspiracy, theft, assault and contract violation."

How could he have guessed? With all the billions of planets, the trillions of people—it wasn't possible!

Gotz read my thoughts. "The red clay under your fingernails; I noticed it the day we met in Junglabesh. In all my travels through the galaxy I'd seen it only once before, on an asteroid called Slabour where children mined red clay with their fingers. You see, Stefin, Serendipity Pharmaceuticals happens to be a subsidiary of Nova Industries."

I glanced at my hands. So long ago—but the faint red crescents were still visible.

"I wasn't sure, of course," Gotz continued. "Your reluctance to discuss your past added to my suspicions. Then last week I had my secretary contact Serendipity Pharmaceuticals. Apparently a Digger had vanished several weeks before our meeting on Junglabesh. The description jibed and DNA prints taken when you acquired your Nova stock confirmed it."

"Look," I said, "what difference does it make? I didn't kill anyone. I didn't really steal anything—except my freedom. What's it matter? Couldn't we just pretend—?"

"You underestimate your own importance, Stefin-Dae."

"What importance?"

Suddenly the words of the Urs came back to me: *Your knowledge of the golden ropes is dangerous . . . a threat to the economic chains that bind the human spirit . . . beware the secrets of synchronicity . . .*

"I saved your life!" I shouted at the vu-screen. "I put you back on the throne!"

"In return," Gotz said calmly, "charges will be dropped against Alan-Tal. He will have his freedom—as long as he remains on Nova Center. He will be given *interesting* work with sufficient remuneration to support the Netts in . . . *a really nice style.*" There was more than a little mockery in his voice. "He will tell the Netts that you left in my yacht for points unknown. He may apologize for you for not having said goodbye or fabricate any other politenesses he sees fit. However, if he mentions so much as a word of what actually went on here, Je-Nett will . . . suffer. You watched Urtz-Al's execution? Then you know that I do not speak lightly."

"I won't do it," Alan said. He stuck out his chin. "Torture me, kill me. I won't desert Stefin!"

"Don't be a borsel," I said. "Go."

"I won't."

The door slid open. Two palace guards entered. They marched over to Alan and grabbed his arms, and he twisted free of them and started kicking them in the shins. Quite a little scuffle ensued. Finally Gotz called from the vu-screen:

"Guards! Leave him be. Bring me the woman Je-Nett instead."

"Wait a minute," Alan said. He looked from me, to the vu-screen, to the guards, and back to me again. He looked so confused I felt sorry for him.

"For God's sake," I said, "get out of here! You'll be happy with Je-Nett. And whatever's waiting for me, I've got to face it alone."

For a full thirty seconds he thought. Then he said, "All right."

The guards reached for his arms, but he shook them loose.

He straightened his caftan—they'd mussed it some—and walked over to me, and took my hand in both of his.

"Goodbye, Stefin. I'll hate myself for the rest of my life for doing this."

"Alan, you don't have any choice. You mustn't feel guilty. Kiss Je-Nett for me."

He gazed at me a moment longer, then he turned and left with the guards. And I was alone with the vu-screen image of Gotz.

"Will you have me killed?"

"I'm afraid I'll have to. But I'll make it as quick and as painless as possible."

"It's got to do with the golden ropes, doesn't it?"

Gotz nodded.

"And the secrets of Synchronicity?"

"Yes."

"It seems like a puzzle where I know all the pieces—but I can't fit them together."

"You would sooner or later. If you lived long enough."

"Condemned men get a last request, don't they? Then that's my last request. How do the pieces fit together? What are the secrets of Synchronicity?"

"When we were on Junglabesh," Gotz began, "I spoke of the Great Corporate Revolution of 2412. Now I will tell you how it came about. Two centuries earlier curious 'crimps' in space were discovered—we call them warp-routes—allowing mankind to populate the galaxy, and relieving the badly crowded star system, Sol, where he originated. There followed the greatest period of expansion and exploration the human race had ever known, and along with it the most radical change in human consciousness since Descartes.

"For the first time man had a realization of the true *vastness* of the galaxy. He settled on planets where Sol could not be seen, even with the aid of a telescope. He came face to face with alien life forms terrifyingly different from himself—creatures like the Urs, for example, to whom technology was a children's game. The warp-routes themselves were disturbing, for they violated every known principle of physics. Men traveled them daily, yet no one could offer the feeblest theory of why they opened where they did, or how they bridged ten thousand light-years of space in a second. The human mind has a terrible need to *explain*. When it can neither explain nor ignore, it must change.

"And change it did, from a materialistic consciousness to a

spiritual one; from the objectivity scientific to the intuitively mystical. For many this meant a return to superstition, a primitive religiosity including idol worship and magic. But a select few, by studying the esoteric techniques of the ancients, achieved miraculous control over mind and body. They learned to heal with 'blessings' and to see in a limited way into the future. They learned to separate the 'ghost' from their physical bodies and train it to travel between the stars on ladders of golden ropes, invisible to all but the adept. They were a small group—true knowledge is always confined to a small group—yet they were respected and revered by the rest of the galaxy.

"The trouble began when this sect, the Wanderers, discovered during their travels through space a *Lapis*—a psychic energizer like the power stone of the Urs—which would increase the psychic powers of *all* mankind if properly distributed. The Lapis was of gigantic proportions, the size of an asteroid. It would allow every man freedom from his body, and from the triviality of everyday life. All well and good. It would also *destroy the capitalist system* which had been so carefully developed and perfected after thousands of years.

"Obviously the spacecraft industry would be the first to go. Who needs spaceships when a man can travel anywhere, instantly, at will? The steel and plastics industries, so reliant on it, would collapse along with it, and electronics would follow shortly. There would also be a subtler effect. The economy of the empire depended to a large extent on 'frustration' buying—the purchasing of unnecessary items as an acting out of sexual and creative frustrations. If the Lapis were distributed to mankind, psychologists predicted, these drives would be fulfilled. Frustration buying would come to an end, and the economy of the galaxy would fall to ruin.

"A terrible war ensued. The UltraCap army, a hundred million strong, battled the ten thousand Wanderers for control of the Lapis. The UltraCaps were armed with the most sophisticated technological weaponry; the Wanderers possessed remarkable occult powers. After a hundred years of killing and destruction the UltraCaps, by virtue of sheer number, had annihilated every last one of the Wanderers—"

"Including," I said, "their general, Bode-Satva."

"Then you've seen the little church. It is the only vestige of prerevolutionary mysticism. We brought them to Nova so we could keep an eye on them. They're harmless enough;

they've degenerated into empty ritual, as religions do after a few thousand years.

"After the war," Gotz continued, "steps were taken to prevent the situation from recurring. All records were destroyed. History was taught only to those at the highest echelon of corporate power, whose loyalty was beyond question. Every time an alien race was encountered that practiced some form of mysticism—and there were many, surprisingly many—they were annihilated lest their teachings be communicated to man. Likewise for any man who seemed to possess mystical knowledge, or the seeds of it. That is the true reason you must die, Stefin—not because of your crimes on Slabour."

"And the Lapis," I said, "what became of it?"

"You still haven't guessed?" Gotz looked amused. "Stefin, I'm surprised! After the UltraCaps took possession of the Lapis, they put their best scientists to work, trying to find a use for it that would not destroy the economy of the galaxy. They discovered that a minute dose did not sufficiently energize the psyche to allow astral travel—but it did create a harmony with the universe which manifested itself in the form of *luck*. If a man were working on a problem and he took this small dose of the Lapis, the solution would be suggested to him by miraculous coincidences, a word overheard from a conversation, a book falling open to a certain page. If a man were trapped in a burning building a small dose of the Lapis might result in a rainstorm quenching the flames, or a handy means of escape presenting itself. In other words, it 'tuned' one to the universe, it improved the odds for a lucky coincidence a millionfold."

Understanding came to me like a blinding light.

"The Lapis," I said, "is Slabour."

Ben-Gotz nodded.

One piece was still missing. "Then why aren't the Diggers lucky? They're always touching the crystals."

"Yes, that was one of the problems that had to be solved before Slabour could be mined. UltraCap scientists developed a material to block the power of the stone, a red clay composed of certain rare minerals. They coated Slabour with it the way a live wire is insulated with plastic. The mining itself posed a trickier problem. A machine was developed, a ray which neutralized the power of the stone for eighteen hours."

"The *Locator*."

He nodded.

"The gunk used to transport the crystals to Romine 3 was

also insulating material. And the refining process consisted, quite simply, in cleaning off the crystals and packaging them in insulated vials. Now your final request has been granted. Your death, as I said, will be as quick and as painless as possible. The cell will be filled with a soporific gas. You will grow drowsy and fall asleep. You will not reawake."

"One more thing."

"What?" He sounded impatient. I was another unpleasant detail to be disposed of as quickly as possible—nothing more.

"Why is it so important to maintain UltraCap?"

"Because," Ben-Gotz said, "that is what we believe in."

The screen went blank.

A hissing sound. Looking up, I saw a white gas seeping through the vent. Before it could reach me I filled my lungs to bursting, then I held my breath and snapped open the wrist of my bionic hand. The vial of Synch drug was rust-red, no bigger than the first joint of my finger. I cracked it along the indentation and saw the liquid inside pulsing with a blue light, like the stone of the Urs, but dimmer. Then pouring it on my tongue, tasteless and cold, painfully cold; the coldness moving down my throat and making a knot in my gut; then radiating like an icy sun throughout my body, to the tips of my fingers and soles of my feet; and finally the peace, the euphoria. Through the gray walls of the cell the golden ropes became visible; though I hadn't the power to travel them, still I could feel them coalescing at my solar plexus, aligning me with the currents which dictate human fortune.

I was so overwhelmed by the feeling, I forgot to hold my breath and took in a lungful of gas. A drowsiness came over me—the golden ropes shimmered and vanished and I was staggering, knees weak, wishing for sleep. It was so seductive, sleep and death and an end to it all, but I fought it, searching inside myself for the energy of the Synch drug. And then I was awake again and the golden ropes were even more vivid than before.

A rumbling. The earth shook, the lights flickered. Dust and chips of stone rained down on me. The rumbling increased and a crack appeared along one wall, traversing it like a snake. Then, to my wonder, the wall split open, forming a crevice just wide enough to admit me. No sooner had I crawled into it than another rumble brought the ceiling tumbling down, leaving me no choice but to continue along the crevice. I squirmed ahead on my stomach, ripping my knees and my forearms, scraping my head, so small was the crawl space. The air was musty and thick with dust. Every breath left me choking. And all around was blackness. I could see nothing, but I felt the golden ropes leading me on through the bowels of the planet.

I don't know how long I squirmed along the crevice—time had ceased—but then I came to a place where it opened onto a tunnel. The airbus driver had spoken of Nova's rich mineral deposits; the planet was honeycombed with mine tunnels, and my synchronistic "earthquake" had delivered me into one! It was high enough for me to stand upright, wide enough for me to run. I leaped the stones that tumbled in my path, and squeezed to the right where a wall on the left had fallen. The ropes of power guided me past all obstacles.

Far, far ahead, a point of light. I didn't feel relief, for I'd felt no distress. From the moment I had swallowed the Synch drug I had known with uncanny certainty that I would survive. I ran along and the light grew brighter. Soon I could see the rough walls of the tunnel, the tamped floor.

Now the light was above me, a vertical shaft penetrating the roof of the tunnel, a distant circle of blue with clouds rushing across it. At one side of the shaft stood a ladder of metal tubes lashed with cord, a makeshift, rickety affair. I began to climb, knowing the ladder would hold, for the ropes of power ascended along with me. I climbed and the circle of light grew bigger, and I climbed and the sounds of the world reached down to me. And then I was at the top of the shaft, breathing the sweet fresh air while friendly hands helped me into the sunlight.

"Welcome back, beloved Bode-Satva!"

Brother Sava-Nanda fell to his knees and started kissing the hem of my filthy caftan.

I was in the Valley of the Workers, at the foot of the Church of Bode-Satva. The shaft from which I had just emerged was the hole they had been digging months ago—coincidence so outrageous I could scarcely believe it! But why had he called me Bode-Satva? And why were the six other monks prostrate at my feet? Then I remembered the Holy Tape:

> "The moment draws near ...
> The day of my return ...
> Dig into the earth where I am buried
> Like a precious jewel ..."

Was it possible? Could they actually believe that I, Stefin-
Dae, was . . .?

"Listen," I said, "I'm not your Bode-Satva!"

"You do not remember," Sava-Nanda said gently. "It is
difficult to remember our former incarnations. But you are
he."

"I took a Synch drug and this is part of a synchronistic sequence, meaningless coincidence, don't you understand?"

"Nothing is meaningless, there are no accidents. Today we
play penultimate Holy Tape #168,895. Bode-Satva say:

> " 'The seed sleeps in the earth.
> When all hope is gone it
> Sends forth green shoots, it
> Bears fruit and the truth is reborn.
>
> Like the seed I rise from earth
> A stranger to myself like every man.
> Yet the fruit of truth is within me
> Awaiting the harvest.
> Om Shanti.' "

Brother Sava-Nanda turned his smile on me.

"You see, it is as prophesied, oh beloved Bode-Satva."

"Please, don't call me that. My name's Stefin."

Wait a minute. What was I doing, standing here, having
just escaped execution and a minor earthquake, trying to con-
vince seven monks that I wasn't some character who'd been
dead for four hundred years? Craziness! Insanity!

"I don't have time for this," I said. "I've got to get out of
here—they'll be after me."

"In ship," Sava-Nanda said. "We take joyful flight, liberate
Lapis, free all mankind!"

"A ship? Yes, but where?"

"Here." Sava-Nanda pointed to the ancient spaceship
church.

"You have to be kidding," I said. "That heap won't fly. It's
lousy with metal fatigue, and there's a crack in the engine
shielding."

"Have faith, will fly. Climb in."

Faith. Faith was all very well, but it wouldn't lift two
hundred tons of broken-down spacecraft. Still, the church
might be a good place to hide until I could figure out what to

do next. I climbed in the hatch and the seven monks followed.

We crossed the bulkhead where religious services had been held, where tableaus of Bode-Satva's life decorated the walls, and we crowded into the elevator, all eight of us. The monks lowered their eyes in my presence, although as we ascended I caught one regarding me with reverence and a little awe. I stared back, irritated. He didn't mind—he was shameless, like a child who has not yet learned what the adult world expects of him.

The elevator opened onto a control deck. Class C shuttles like this ship were the largest vessels ever constructed for atmospheric flight. While the small shuttles I'd ridden in barely accommodated two in the cockpit, the control deck here was spacious, individual loungers and consoles for captain, co-pilot, space navigator, warp navigator, communications officer and so forth. Impressive equipment, but I doubted if any of it was still operational.

I followed the monks to an alcove containing a wooden chest oramented with gold filigree and studded with jewels. They knelt before it, dipping their heads and circling their hearts, but I remained standing—I'd never knelt to anybody or anything, least of all a box, and I didn't intend to start now. Then Sava-Nanda opened the chest and presented me with its sole contents: a flight tape.

On the tape reel had been painted, in excruciating detail, a scene of Bode-Satva lashed to the five-spoked wheel, surrounded by all sorts of mythical beasts and gods, a fire-breathing dragon and an eight-armed woman, a man with the head of an elephant and a winged lambit. The paint was cracked and peeling—it must have predated the ship, and perhaps it was as old as old Bode-Satva himself.

"Very nice," I said. "Good painting."

"It is the Holy Program for the Final Voyage. It needs your blessing."

Oh hell. This made me extremely uncomfortable. But if I was going to take refuge here, I should respect their wishes.

I raised the tape and said, "I hereby bless this tape."

"Om Shanti," they said.

"Om Shanti," I agreed.

"Now please insert in autopilot."

Obediently I pushed the tape into a slot in the captain's console. Then, playing along with the charade, I buckled into the captain's lounger—after all, I was the Bode-Satva—while

Sava-Nanda and another monk, Manas-Ananda, performed the preflight check. This Manas-Ananda seemed to be the pilot of the group, although I found it difficult to believe that such a gay, plump little man could run a ship when all the other pilots I'd known had been lean and hard and steely-eyed. Of course running a ship that wouldn't fly was a simpler matter than running one that would.

To my amazement the instruments came to life, vu-screens painting our course in livid electric colors, indicator needles jiggling, LEDs flashing their count-down numbers:

Fifteen—fourteen—thirteen . . .

But it didn't really mean a thing—electrical equipment could withstand the years, mechanical equipment could not. There was no chance of the engines still being operational. And whatever the half-life of the fuel, it had to be mostly decayed by now.

Twelve—eleven—ten—nine . . .

When this countdown failed they'd probably have another, and possibly a third before admitting defeat. I'd commiserate. Then, after sundown, I'd ask one of the monks to deliver a message to Alan.

Eight—seven—six—five . . .

With his help I could get to the spaceport undetected, sneak aboard a ship wearing some kind of disguise.

Four—three—two . . .

Better still, we could hire a land sled, drive up to the polar cap and reclaim Gotz's yacht, then . . .

One—ignition.

Oh my God, the ship shuddering and shaking, every steel seam screaming in protest. Another earthquake—or were we struggling from the grip of father gravity who clings so when his children come to visit? Could that long-decayed fuel still create fusion? Could those ancient alloy chambers still contain the stream of plasma, hot as a star's heart? No, it had to be an earthquake—but there was the acceleration flattening me to the lounger, squeezing the breath out of me as if I were a tube of nutrients. The pressure, the strain, the shaking—too much, teetering on the ledge of consciousness, I tumbled into blackness and quiet, blessed relief.

"Bode-Satva? Bode-Satva?"

The monks were standing in a circle around my lounger, smiling down on me.

"Passed out," I said, rubbing my eyes.

They smiled some more. What sweet, gentle people. Then they gave me a pair of magnetic sandals to keep my feet on the floor and I followed them to the elevator.

We descended to another deck, where supper was served at a long table, vegetables stuck to a platter with a sauce that burned my tongue and made my eyes water.

"Where," I asked Manas-Ananda, "are we headed?"

"To the Lapis, naturally."

Slabour. The memory of the asteroid from where my long journey had begun made my palms sweat.

"Can our course be altered?"

"No. The Holy Program for the Final Voyage is immutable."

Well, I had intended to return to Slabour anyway and bring justice to the Diggers. But my plans had always been vague, consigned to the hazy future. Now it appeared that, assuming metal fatigue did not turn the ship into a hydrogen bomb over the next few months, I would have need for concrete actions far sooner than I had ever hoped or imagined. Justice for the Diggers—simple enough to say. Concocting a step-by-step plan was more difficult. I hadn't, as a matter of fact, a notion of where to begin.

"When we reach the Lapis," I said to Sava-Nanda, "how exactly will we liberate it?"

"You do not know?" He looked surprised. Then he grinned. "No matter. Solution will present itself."

"Perhaps on final Holy Tape," another monk offered. He was Brother Shravana-Ananda, the communications officer, and his big ears and buck teeth would have made him positively comical if not for the beauty of his innocence, a beauty they all shared. He continued, "Knowing you would not remember, you probably left yourself a reminder."

"But what if I didn't know back then that . . . ?" Uh-oh, now I was doing it too. Quickly I corrected myself. "I mean, we don't really know if Bode-Satva knew that I wouldn't know."

"You knew," Sava-Nanda said. He took a bite of radishflower and explained: "Time and his sister space are product of physical perceptions. In *real* world they not exist. No time, no space. All at once! Sometimes when world very beautiful, we have glimpses of it, we say, *Ah-ha! timeless moment*. Bode-Satva transcends physical perceptions, sees all past and future as now. Sees himself trying to remember how to liberate Lapis. Gives himself clue. You see."

There was a paradox in there someplace. Maybe I could figure it out if my mind wasn't so muddy.

"No more worry," he said, watching me mulling over it. "Everything be fine. Now eat up, grow strong."

He handed me a carrotchoke.

10

We assembled on the main deck to witness Holy Tape #168,896—the last of the Holy Tapes. We sat crosslegged in a semicircle around the vu-screen while Brother Sava-Nanda inserted the cassette. And once again I was gazing at the image of Bode-Satva, regal yet benevolent upon his high carved throne. The halo of frizzy black hair, the liquid eyes, the smile that penetrated to my very heart. Was I imagining it, or did some ancient memory stir within me like a hibernating creature under the first melt of spring? No, if I entertained the possibility for even an instant, I might start believing it, and if I believed it I would have to consider myself insane. Or preposterous.

"The final tape, the last words
Of self gone
To self reborn
Across the temporal chasm.

You do not recall
For the mind's lens is clouded
And cannot perceive the truth.
Wash it clear with tears of pain.

Even God weeps. His fine cool rain
Will rinse the Lapis free from dust
And all who mine will thus acquire
Synchronistic fortune,
Freedom from the flesh.

Generous souls, they shall disburse
The stone throughout the galaxy
Drowning the merchants of misery
In a sea of bliss. Then all will be
As it should be and as it must.
And man will make a millimeter move
Closer to almighty God.
Om Shanti."

The monks dipped their heads and circled their hearts. Sava-Nanda raised the tape in his palm. With a sound like a gasp it turned to powder and swirled away, a tiny dust-devil.

All is transient—even the word of Bode-Satva."

No matter how much they acknowledged transience, I could feel their melancholy at the passing of four hundred and sixty years of tradition. Never again would the voice of Bode-Satva echo through the meeting deck, never again would his image grace the vu-screen. So we sat there savoring the end of it, meditating upon the final words, until Brother Sava-Nanda spoke.

"It is as I said. Bode-Satva remembers that he has forgotten. He sends himself answer across time. Now you understand." Noticing my puzzlement, his own conviction wavered. "Don't you?"

"Some of it." I explained about Slabour and the Diggers and the red clay.

"There!" Sava-Nanda said, triumphantly. "Rains come to Slabour, wash away clay. Energized by Lapis, Diggers become like Wanderers of ancient. Help you spread salvation across galaxy. So simple! So beautiful! Truly Bode-Satva's planning is faultless, his prescience unerring! Om Shanti!"

The other monks Om Shanti-ed back and circled their hearts and hugged each other with joy.

"Except for one thing," I said with annoyance. "It doesn't rain on Slabour. It never has and it never will."

"Again you doubt your powers. You escape through hole you order us to dig—then say, *No, no, meaningless coincidence!*"

The other monks chuckled at his impression of me.

"You tell us church will not fly," he continued, "and you launch us on our heavenly journey. Now you say no rain on Lapis, but—"

"The difference is," I interrupted, "the coincidence with the hole was caused by the Synch drug, and as for the church, well, it was more spaceworthy than it looked from the outside. But there is *no way* rain will fall on Slabour."

"There is atmosphere, yes?" Sava-Nanda was questioning me as if I were some thick-skulled child. "There is water to drink? There are human bodies, most part water? Then there is water to rain!"

"*No there isn't water to rain!*"

How exasperating! I wanted to grab them by their saffron robes and shake them out of their bliss and tell them that you had to take care of yourself in this galaxy—no cosmic daddies were standing by to save you from your own stupidity. I wanted to tell them, these trusting children who'd never felt the sting of betrayal, about ads in the Daily Tape offering boys all-expense-paid round-trip spaceflights that never returned, and execupimps who promised to buy contraband Creelium, and brave, brave 'barian hunters and interstellar realtors, and corporate heads who turned people into chess machines and rewarded favors with endless sleep in underground cells . . .

But before I could speak they were filing into the elevator, on their way to the dining deck to celebrate mankind's salvation with the last remaining keg of Bode-Satva's spittle. Oh damn, what difference did it make? Let them enjoy a moment of triumph after four hundred and sixty years of waiting, for in a few months' time their faith would crumble to a handful of rust-red dust.

11

One of the monks summoned me to the control deck—a
matter of the utmost urgency, he said. Arriving, I found the
rest of them crowded around Shravana-Nanda's lounger,
watching him fiddle frantically with the dials of his console.
When he saw me he slipped off his headset.

"Bode-Satva, I am receiving a tachyon transmission from
Nova Center."

He flipped a tumbler, rerouting the signal through a large
wall speaker. Beneath the hiss and crackle I could discern
voices, like bright fish at the bottom of a muddy pond.

"What language are they speaking? I can't understand a
word of it."

"Primary Galactic," Shravana-Nanda replied. "But it is
scrambled—and that is why I suspect importance."

"Can you unscramble it?"

"Can try."

So we stood around the console for nearly twenty minutes
watching him squint and scowl and run his tongue around
the inside of his mouth, while he fooled with the dials. Then,
bit by bit an impish grin spread across his face; he winked
at me.

"Modesty aside, I am pretty good breaking scramble. Listen:"

*Buzz hiss Nova Center to Slabour Mining Camp hiss
crackle in please errrr fugitive Digger Stefin pop to breep
control of Slabour crackle crackle anti-UltraCap faction errrr
maybe armed with heavy artillery repeat burrr heavy hiss
crackle best possibility halting attempt according to buzz hiss
profile compiled by Nova wreeep will be to arrange passage
for pop crackle breeep to Slabour and use eeyow for bargain-
ing position over pop buzz hiss crackle breeep. . . .*

"Useful information," I said.

Shravana-Nanda beamed.

12

I lay in my hammock staring up at the ceiling. Someone had tacked a five-spoked wheel up there so it would be the first sight in the morning, the last at night. I had been staring at it without interruption for the last three hours and feeling no more holy for the experience. I would have preferred going to sleep, but a fine panic about tomorrow kept me in a state of wide-eyed, sweat-sopped, heart-thudding wakefulness.

Tomorrow we would land on Slabour.

There was no avoiding it. The Holy Program for the Final Voyage had been automatically locked into the autopilot, almost as though old Bode-Satva had taken precautions, knowing I wouldn't go unless I had to. Slabour. My mind reared away from it like a frightened borsel. If only we had some weapons—but the monks didn't believe in weapons. Not even a power laser on board. And as for that sudden thunderstorm, well, it would indeed be a miracle.

Rain. Was there any way . . . ? Well, it wouldn't hurt to ask the computer. Anything better than lying here working myself into a fit. Any action better than this terrible feeling of helplessness.

I slipped my toes into my magnetic sandals and pulled a caftan over my head. Then I clacked out to the elevator.

The control deck was deserted, dark but for the signal lights blinking abstract patterns of color in slow soothing rhythms. Dropping into the captain's lounger, I requested an encyclopedic function and in a few seconds the small vu-screen on my console began to print:

ENCYCLOPEDIC FUNCTION
REQUEST TOPIC

"Is there any way to make rain?"

REPHRASE REQUEST IN ONE
WORD IF POSSIBLE

"Rainmaking."

The printing was replaced by a picture of a man standing on a sand dune, staring at the sky, shading his eyes from a blazing sun. He looked miserable, and lest there be any doubt, high-pitched, scraping music of the most painful sort let me share his discomfort.

"Rain," an announcer said, "wet, refreshing and wonderful! Rain. Nature's way of turning a desert world into a lush greensward. If you're interested in irrigating your planet *nature's way*, then you're interested in WeatherMaker's CloudBurster X-3, the newest, most revolutionary concept in rainmakers."

Magically a crate appeared next to the man; he opened it and lifted out a small rocket on a tripod launcher. In less than a minute the "easy-to-launch CloudBurster X-3" was burning a trail across the sky.

A title card appeared:

ONLY FIVE DAYS LATER . . .

Then the man dancing like a lunatic in the downpour, catching water in his hands and pouring it over his head, drinking it straight from the sky while every manner of green plant sprouted at his feet.

"Contact WeatherMakers for further information. Cloud-Bursters begin at 87,959 CUs. Six to eight months' wait for delivery."

"Wonderful," I said. "Rainmaking," I continued, "*without* a Cloudburster X-3."

THREE METHODS (A) SPRAYING WARM
(60 PLUS F) CLOUDS WITH WATER (B)
INFUSING COLD CLOUDS (27 TO 5 F)
WITH DRY ICE OR WITH (C) SILVER
IODIDE CRYSTALS CAUTION OVERSEEDING
MAY DISSIPATE CLOUDS NOTE ALL THREE
TECHNIQUES OF LIMITED EFFICACY.

"Cancel," I said, and linking my fingers behind my head, leaned back to think it over. One of those techniques might be practical—even if it was of "limited efficacy." And, for all I knew, Slabour might have clouds hidden in her dust-thick sky. And the clouds might be of the proper warmth. And I might turn into a purple Kimba bear with blue polka-dots.

13

Slabour. It hung like a lump of clotted blood in the vu-screen, half afire in its artificial sun, half invisible in shadow.

"Prepare to land, Captain?" Manas-Ananda asked me.

He was strapped into the lounger next to mine, and the other monks were stationed around us, performing the pre-entrance operations like a practiced team.

"The Holy Program for the Final Voyage," I said, "is it still guiding us?"

"No—we just changed to manual."

"Aha. In that case instead of landing I think we should fly on to the nearest large planet where we can purchase a CloudBurster X-3 rainmaking machine. It'll take six to eight months for delivery. Meanwhile, we can work out plans—"

"No more fuel," Manas-Ananda apologized. "Must land."

"Go ahead then," I gloomily conceded. I felt so stupid and helpless, like a krombar wandering into a roasting pit an hour before dinner. "One thing: What do we have in the water tanks?"

"A thousand gallons," said the monk who was monitoring life-support systems.

"Is there an external drain? Can we empty the tanks when we come into the atmosphere? I'd like to spray out all the water at twelve thousand feet."

"Maximize tank pressure," Manas-Ananda said thoughtfully, "open outside fill-valve a crack—yes, can be done but very dangerous."

"Do it," I said.

"Bode-Satva," Shravana-Nanda called, "I am receiving transmission from Slabour. Will you listen? Or disregard?"

"Run it on the side-screen, and proceed with entrance."

Here I was, I who had been halfway across the galaxy and back; who had a half-dozen times slipped away from the icy fingers of death; who had spoken telepathically with aliens and roamed the astral plane and won and lost a hundred

161

thousand CUs—and despite it all, the pudgy arrogant face on the vu-screen made my heart race and my hands turn clammy with fear.

"Stefin dear, can you hear me? It's your old friend Callow."

"I can hear you."

"My, but it's been a long time! I've heard the most outrageous things about you. Ben-Gotz called me from Nova—he says you've become quite the little terrorist, and you're determined to take Slabour. Stefin, I don't know if you realize the gravity of what you intend to do. Slabour is the most important piece of *real estate* in the galaxy—why, in the universe for that matter! If every common citizen takes a piece of it, willy-nilly, chaos would reign! People simply aren't ready for this kind of power. Let's just say we are *guarding* it until they are ready—holding it in safekeeping.

"Now, don't think I underestimate you, Stefin. You're a smart lad. As a matter of fact, you're executive material. If you'll land peacefully and forget about this nonsense of *liberating the Lapis*, we'll enroll you in our executive training corps. You'll become a Vice-Prez, Stefin, maybe even a Prez! A privileged citizen of the galaxy. You'll have all the comforts you could imagine—lovely women, enormous wealth. Power. Respect."

"Forget it," I said. "I'm not interested." And I wasn't just being noble. Callow's promises, true or not, held no allure.

He squeezed his lips in a pout, and his eyes spoke awful disappointment in me.

"Dear Stefin," he said, "it hurts me to do this—but really! You leave me no other choice."

His face was replaced by a view of a bright little room lined with instrument banks. A chair was bolted to the floor and in it, clamped by her slim ankles and wrists, with a belt around her chest and a helmet cutting into her mane of soft black hair, sat Suki, her lovely face twisted into a grimace of sheer horror.

"And she will remain in the LAS," Boss Callow said, "until we have you in captivity."

14

"Do you still want me to drain the water tanks?" Manas-Ananda asked, after Callow had ended transmission.

"Whatever you want," I said. "It doesn't matter now. Nothing matters."

Part VII

Epilogue

1

Twelve security guards were waiting when we opened the hatch. They handcuffed us together by the wrist, like paper dolls. I told them we had nothing, no guns, no bombs; they didn't believe me. They frisked us thoroughly and two stayed behind to search the ship while the others led us down the rough clay path to the Administration Tower.

We passed some Diggers straggling back from the mines; I knew one of them.

"Mo?"

He squinted in my direction. His eyes lit on me for an instant, then moved on to the other monks and the guards. I guess he didn't recognize me. Two years is a long time.

"Mo," I called, "it's me, Ste—"

"No talking!" barked the guard and the butt of his stinger came down *whack* across my shoulder blades. I stumbled and the monks on either side stopped to help me up.

"Keep walking!" shouted the guard.

I was back on Slabour, all right.

Boss Callow was waiting in his room on the top floor of the tower. He lay on his lounger, pale and bloated like a dead fish, regarding us with amusement. Then he ordered the guards to separate us and lock the monks in individual detention cells. I was to remain with him.

"I'm sorry," I said to Brother Sava-Nanda. "You see, I'm not your Bode-Satva."

"You are! Liberation will be soon, no despair."

Faithful to the last—how I admired them. They all smiled at me and Om Shanti-ed until the guards shoved them into the hall. Two guards stayed behind. They kept their eyes on me and their hands on their stingers.

"Where's Suki?" I demanded.

"She'll be here shortly," Callow said. "The medic is *preparing* her."

His eyes twinkled with hints of some marvelous surprise. I stared back at him and after a while he looked away.

"Ah, Stefin," he sighed. "Stefin, Stefin, Stefin. Who'd have thought you'd turn out to be such a troublemaker?"

Then the medic came in, leading a hobbled old woman by the wrist. She wore a plain, loose-fitting black dress and heavy black shoes. Her hair was a tangle of black and silver. Her head was lowered, her face covered by a bony arm from which the flesh hung like a hammock. She drew back, but the medic pushed her forward until she stood only a foot or two from me.

I glanced at Callow, puzzled.

He rose from the lounger and stepped up behind her. He pulled back her arms and held them with one hand, and he slipped the other hand under her chin to force up her head. Her skin was loose and wrinkled, but I recognized the high cheekbones and the strong chin, and I recognized the imploring eyes gazing at me from within.

"Suki . . . ?"

Her voice was gravelly. "Don't look at me!"

"What did you do to her?" I screamed at Callow.

He started to laugh.

I got in one good punch, right across the face, before the security guards caught me by the arms and pulled me away.

Callow touched the blood pouring from his mouth. He wasn't laughing any more.

"Lock them up together," he said. "It's their wedding night. Tomorrow I'll think of a special treat for the honeymoon."

2

Dusk turned the detention cell crimson, and the bars set into the windows cast long black stripes across the floor. Suki huddled in the corner, her face away from me. I bent over and stroked her back. She shivered at the touch.

"Go away. Leave me alone."

"It's the Change, isn't it? The Youthification wore off—but how could it happen so quickly? When I saw you in the LAS you were still—"

"They made the tape weeks ago. Since then the medic's been giving me injections to speed up the Change. Boss Callow thought it would be a good joke on you."

"The joke's on him. I don't care."

Gently I turned her from the wall and raised her face to mine. She pulled away.

"Don't," she said. "Don't pretend."

"I'm not pretending."

I touched her lips and as I did the room exploded with light, as if we'd bridged a circuit; then it was dark again.

"What was that? Stefin, what was it?"

A rumble of thunder. I ran to the window and grabbed the cold bars and pressed my face against them, trying to see into the charcoal night. It came again, another flash, a glaring zigzag etched against the sky and the barracks, the scru-shed, the distant shape of the Church of Bode-Satva all appeared in that instant, bleached of color by the brightness, then vanished again into the night.

Again the thunder, and a new sound, a sound Slabour had never heard: a patter of rain pelting clay. A drizzle at first, then the heavens opened and down it came pouring. In the next flash I saw puddles forming and rivulets running along the low places.

"What's happening, Stefin? Oh, I'm scared."

I held her close and stroked her hair.

"Watch, Suki," I whispered. "It's the end of everything. And the beginning of . . . "

"Of what?"

Another flash. Churning rivers of red clay ground gullies in the earth, cutting deeper and deeper until suddenly a crack of cool blue light appeared, pulsing in rhythm with the universe, casting a web of golden ropes across all bounds of time and space.

"I feel so strange," she murmured. "As though we're starting all over again."

I looked at her and what I saw was the slender spindle of her soul all aglow with light.

"Come," I said.

I took her hand and we began to climb the golden ladder together, to wherever it might lead.

About the Author

Jonathan Fast has written for the movies (*Love Al Dente*, a screenplay he coauthored will soon be a major motion picture from Universal), and for television, and his short stories have been widely anthologized. *The Secrets of Synchronicity*, his first novel to be published, integrates Vedic myths with many of the more traditional elements of science fiction.

He lives in Connecticut with his old lady and his dog, and usually spends part of the year on the Coast. He was once a composer, a child prodigy, and still enjoys playing chamber music with friends. He spends several hours a day practicing Yoga. Science and religion fascinate him equally, and he hopes that by learning all he possibly can about both he will eventually discover that they are two aspects of the same thing. He longs for a cogent universe.